THE
SPACE
GUARDIANS

BRIAN BALL

A POCKET BOOK EDITION published by
Simon & Schuster of Canada, Ltd. • Markham, Ontario, Canada
Registered User of the Trademark

THE SPACE GUARDIANS

Future Publications edition published 1975

POCKET BOOK edition published November, 1975
2nd printing.........September, 1975

Standard Book Number: 671-80198-8.

Printed in Canada.

"Anton!" she screamed above the noise.

He turned, the great grey-black mass of his head pivoting. Painfully slow sounds came from what had once been his mouth.

"E – va!" Two syllables.

"What's happened to you?" she cried, appalled. Eva could see his head now, the metallic body, the tree-like limbs gleaming in the half-light of fission.

And Commander Koenig heard the terrible agony of the thing that had once been Anton Zoref. It crawled now, huge and horrible, dragging itself closer and closer to the controls of the massive nuclear generator. . . .

THE SPACE GUARDIANS
was originally published by Futura Publications Limited.

Books in the Space: 1999 Series

Breakaway
Moon Odyssey
The Space Guardians

Published by POCKET BOOKS

THE
SPACE
GUARDIANS

CHAPTER ONE

Dr Helena Russell looked out over the bleak pinnacles of volcanic rock. She shivered. The reaches of space were so vast, so empty. A star, brighter than most, flared briefly. She turned away. Then she remembered Koenig's advice: 'When it gets bad, Helena, go out and look at it close. The rock. The ash. And the craters. And then look up to the stars. When you do that ask yourself, Are we *really* alone out here? Try it, Helena. Try it.'

She had. Koenig's quiet, reassuring words could soothe her fears most times, but not now. She remembered why. Koenig was away, checking on a reading from the computer. Moonbase Alpha was a different place without John Koenig.

The routine of Medical Centre claimed her attention. A badly-burned crewman needed dressings. Dr Russell was guiltily glad of the chance to lose herself in professional attentions, to forget for a while that they were on a barren rock and heading, out of control, into regions where the star-maps ended.

A hundred miles away, Commander Koenig was thinking along similar lines. Since the nuclear cataclysm which had blown the Moon clear of Earth and into its giddying flight through unchartered space, he had become accustomed to the distances and the emptiness. And the danger. He could accept the tragedies incidental to keeping Moonbase Alpha a going concern.

Nearing a new star system that might hold intelligent life no longer stirred him, for all they had sighted had so far proved to be barren.

Accidents, disappointments, these were constants on Alpha. They could be borne with. But what Koenig could never accept was the glaring truth of their complete and final severance from Earth.

It was a life sentence.

Always to live on the grey ash and dust and rock: always to need machines to survive. It was unthinkable. There had to be a way back. He suppressed a sigh that turned into a yawn. Carter, pilot of the exploratory Eagle, noticed:

'Tired, John?' he asked the Moonbase Commander. All the Eagle's crew were tired. 'You look it. I hate to say it, but it's another useless trip. Ten hours looking for a lode of mineral deposits we can use and nothing to show for our time.'

'Anything, Sandra?' called Koenig.

Koenig wouldn't show what he felt. The technician, Sandra Benes, answered from the passenger module:

'No show, Commander. I've treble-checked the bearing the computer gave us, but there's no sign of the indicated deposits.'

Koenig looked at her, a slim, dark-haired girl who radiated efficiency. If she said her monitors gave a no-show, he believed her.

'The computer was certain,' put in Professor Bergman. 'Strange. We've quartered the co-ordinates for hours.' His thin face looked remote. 'It shouldn't be wrong. John, there *was* a radiation effect. See.'

Carter looked at the clipboard with its shadowy lines. Bergman pressed switches, and the screen reproduced the hazy bluish smear which had got the computer as near excitement as it ever could.

'Here it is, Commander,' said Sandra Benes. She tore off a read-out from the Eagle's computer link.

Bergman was still troubled.

'There *was* an effect. It had a cause. John, how about a freak radiation—'

'Search complete,' called Sandra Benes. Then she noticed that Bergman was talking. Oh, I'm sorry for interrupting, Professor.'

'It's nothing, nothing, Sandra.'

'Well, Victor?' said Koenig.

'A stray thought—nothing firm, John.'

'Head for Moonbase, Commander?' asked Carter.

Koenig still looked at the thin, ascetic face. But Bergman shook his head. 'I'll check it out when we're back,' he said. 'We're wasting time here. I could use some sleep myself.'

'Alan, head for home,' Koenig ordered. 'Eagle One to Alpha.' The screen in front of him blipped and then showed the round face of Paul Morrow at Main Mission Control. 'There's nothing but dust and rock again, Paul.' Koenig hid his disappointment. 'We're heading back.'

Bergman looked out of the forward con. A star-system hung delicately above the rearing jagged horizon ahead. His eyes narrowed. 'Unless—'

And then he gasped in sudden shock as the ship bucked in a tight turn. Carter yelled hoarsely as he was slammed back in his seat. Sandra Benes hurtled towards a bank of monitors and crashed in a shattered heap. Bergman's wiry strength kept him from harm; Carter was in his restraint harness, as regulations demanded.

Koenig saw blank black space as the ship again switch-backed violently.

'Eagle One to Alpha!' he gasped. 'Emergency! Losing control—'

Koenig fastened one strap of the restraint harness. He glimpsed the screen. Blank. The thrust of the ship was too much to allow him to move, but he could see no life in the intercom screen. Then the ship dived in a bewildering, bone-jarring rush.

Bergman was trying to reach the still body of Sandra Benes when the ship dived. His motion continued, sickeningly fast until he lurched into a bulkhead. Then he too crumpled into unconsciousness.

'Power!' Koenig yelled to the pilot. He couldn't reach the dual controls. 'Pull her out, Alan—hold her!'

Ahead, downwards, the grey rocks waited. Koenig heard his own voice and that of Carter. Somewhere behind, the dull sound of bone and flesh thudding on metal.

'It's responding!' Carter croaked. 'She's coming round—'

Koenig was driven back by the forces surging from the Eagle's two engines. He cartwheeled as the ship slid past a mammoth outcrop of black tooth-edged rock. His last memories were of a jolting that shook every plate of the ship; of the jangling sound of metal ripping; of a great well of blackness encompassing the Eagle; and the harness giving and a thrust that propelled him the length of the command module, to slam into the forward con, thinking, 'It shouldn't end like this, not on a grey-black surface—' Then an appalling blow on his head. And that was all: pain and regret, red-blackness, nothing.

The alarm system whined into silence.

'Eagle One! Eagle One!' rapped out the Duty Officer. He knew he was wasting his time. The scanners showed nothing. Eagle One was a wreck: no, Eagle One was a total wreck, with barely enough residual power to show its location.

Paul Morrow assumed command as he was contacting Helena Russell.

'Where? How bad?' he asked tensely.

The Duty Officer pointed to the screen:

'We've got them in a big crater a hundred miles from Alpha, Paul. Weak emissions of power. Their main propulsion unit is out. It was a bad crash—erratic flight, then a cut off. There'll be casualties.'

Kano joined Paul Morrow.

Helena's face appeared on the screen. Morrow saw the piercingly blue eyes full of anguish.

'How bad?' he asked. 'Do you get a reading?'

'I know three are alive, one weak. But Commander Koenig's medical monitor doesn't register, Paul!'

'John!' whispered Kano.

They all had the same thought. Koenig had held them together in the first terrible moments of space-wreck. His sometimes icy detachment had persuaded terrified men and women that they could still hope in spite of the cataclysm which had blotted out all thought of normal life. His essential humanity radiated throughout Moonbase Alpha, a visible life-line for the weak and a constant source of reassurance for the strong.

'Not John,' said Morrow. 'Not John Koenig!' He remembered his duty. 'Dr Russell, prepare a medical team and get over to Launch Pad Seven. I want you on the way in five minutes.'

She felt like running, but she remained calm. Heart racing, she detailed her team. And then she checked the vital life-readings. Three registered. One gave no reading at all.

As the Rescue Eagle soared away from the Moonbase complex, the word filtered throughout its miles of corridors, penetrating to the furthest recess in the deep underground laboratories, store-rooms and workshops. *Commander Koenig bad.* No one dared to name the unspoken thought.

Paul Morrow realized that he was gripping the supports of the command chair too hard. Kano's technicians watched his broad face for a hint of news. He forced himself to remain calm. He must not show panic. Minutes dragged by.

'They must be there!' growled someone irritably.

As if in response, a misty image filled the screen. It showed the rearing pinnacles of black rock and the deep shadows of a gigantic crater.

'I see them!' called the pilot of the Rescue Eagle.

'How's the Commander?' asked Morrow levelly. 'Helena? Dr Russell? What do you have?'

'Still no life-reading,' she said. 'Nothing, Paul. We're going down now.'

Morrow and Kano exchanged glances. It took very little time. The seconds thudded away like strokes from an axe. Then:

'He's alive,' with wonder and relief from Helena Russell. 'He's badly hurt, but he's alive.'

'Thank God,' whispered Morrow. He would have said more, but Helena Russell's voice cut in again:

'We've two casualties, Professor Bergman and Sandra Benes. They're not too bad. But I'm worried about the Commander—will you get David Kano to check with computer?'

'Check what, Dr Russell?' said Kano.

'Check his life-readings. And quickly!'

'Immediately!'

'Why, Dr Russell?' asked Morrow. He kept the new apprehension from his voice.

'Because there's nothing showing on his personal monitor—it's at zero, Paul!'

'But he's alive, Doctor! You said so!'

'Run the check, please, Paul. John Koenig is

breathing. Just. But there is no indication of life apart from that, not according to his body-sensors.'

Paul Morrow knew what she meant. Sensors embedded at the vital areas measured all uses of energy. Now, none of them registered. It must be a technical fault. For life to go on, there had to be the use of energy.

Kano returned.

'Well, David?'

'Computer says the sensors are a hundred per cent.'

Morrow paled. Commander Koenig was breathing. But the computer said he was dead.

CHAPTER TWO

It had been a long walk, but Koenig felt curiously refreshed. If he hadn't known how absurd the idea to be, he could have been striding along a tree-lined road with the wind cutting across grassland and the sun warm on his face. The space-suit hardly worried him, the heavy headpiece rubbed only gently on his shoulders.

He pushed a button and stepped through the airlock. They'd be surprised to see him. Curious that the Rescue Mission had been so long. But they probably had other things to attend to. It hadn't been such a bad crash after all. Bergman and Service Technician Benes injured but not critically. Carter in good spirits even though he had not been able to raise Alpha. Someone had to make the long walk, so Koenig had ordered them to remain with the Eagle.

Koenig pushed off his helmet. The travel tube accelerated and within a minute he was in the corridor which led to Main Mission Control. A sense of urgency filled him now, but also a feeling of well-being. He had survived. There were injuries, but it was not a disaster.

'Paul?' he called, as the door slid away.

A low humming filled the room. Air-circulating fans: a subdued electronic whisper from screens: the sense of power units pumping life into Moonbase. All as it should be. Except that one never noticed the low insistent noise: There was always the sound of the human voice to hide it.

'David!' Koenig heard his own voice ring out into the near-silence.

Main Mission Control was deserted. There was no sign of movement whatsoever. Puzzled, Koenig walked to his office. The door slid back at his touch.

'Paul!'

It was so strange as to be puzzling. Always, there was movement, life, the sounds of human activity. Decisions, questions, small jokes, the common courtesies of their lives. Suddenly, Koenig whirled.

There had been movement. He glimpsed the woman.

'What the devil—' he began, too stunned to finish the expostulations, for the woman was a complete stranger to him and she was already fading in a strange purple haze as he stared open-mouthed at her.

The woman had been there: she was gone.

She was quite tall, slim, dressed in a long gown which shimmered with red and gold lights. It covered her body yet revealed, its beauties. The form beneath had a graceful elegance, rounded and slender: honey-bronze and exquisite. And she had vanished in the moment he had looked at her.

He passed a hand over his forehead. He looked down at the hand. No blood. There had been a cut . . .

He looked at his wrist.

He shivered. Without making a conscious decision, he turned back to his office and ordered a reading on the crew of Eagle One. 'Life-reading,' he said. 'Carter, pilot. Professor Bergman. Technician Benes. He paused. 'And Commander, Moonbase.'

Silently he examined the readings. One normal. Two showed damage, not serious. One: nothing. 'Re-check on Commander Koenig!' he snapped, unable to keep the raw edge of tension from his voice.

'Correct readings, sir,' said a smooth electronic voice. There was no surprise in it, nothing but cold efficiency.

Koenig looked down at the wrist which had attracted his attention when he tried to wipe off the blood which should have issued from the wound. The life-register indicators showed nothing: a nil reading.

The computer confirmed the information.

Koenig trembled. He felt panic begin to scream through his mind, and then he realized that he, of all people, could not abandon himself to despair. He forced himself to walk carefully through to Main Mission Control. There was a mystery here but it could be explained. Always, there had to be an explanation.

But the silence? The deserted Control? The nil reading?

He crossed to the big scanner.

'General view,' he said.

The scanners in orbit over the Moon would show him Moonbase, pinpoint any aberrations and pick out the cause of the mystery. For there had to be cause. Something threatened Moonbase. They would read the signs and pick out the intertwining agency.

The scanner blazed instantly, flooding with a deep violet-purple. And then images formed. Koenig reeled. The impact was tremendous. A city filled the screen. It could be nothing else. Human, undoubtedly made for people. But how could people make such things? Dazzling shapes, iridescent under a calm and brilliant purple sky, but shapes which changed as you looked at them—colours spangling and coruscating like living things, and then turning back into regular shapes as tiny craft darted in amongst them, to hang and then become absorbed.

Koenig knew that, without question, he was looking into the future of his race. Even as he began to ask the dazed questions which sprang into his mind, the city (*city?* thought Koenig, but like *that?*) became part of a shifting, more subtle, panorama. Koenig reached for the console and strained against vertigo.

Blue and purple particles spun before him. There was a sense of darkness, of impossible distances and unimaginable speed. And then, slowly, a figure took shape. A man, thought Koenig. *One from our future.*

He was tall, as tall as Koenig, wide-shouldered and confident. Younger than me, thought Koenig, and this was strange too, for the man's eyes were heavy with knowledge, experience, and power.

'Welcome to Zenno, Commander,' he said.

CHAPTER THREE

'Gently, Commander,' he warned. 'Think. It is real, not a dream. This is a planet. I exist, just as you do.'

Koenig began to recover from his bewildered stupe-faction as he put his right hand to his head. There had been a blow. The crash. That was it. Crashed, a concussion, and now hallucination.

The man shook his head.

'No, Commander. This is a planet. Its existence won't be suspected by your race for a hundred of your life-times. Perhaps never.' The smile, thought Koenig, betrayed the man, *arrogant*.

'I had a computer check on all the star-systems in this sector. Not one has a habitable planet.'

'Commander, we can camouflage our existence from your archaic probes.'

Archaic, thought Koenig. He thinks we're back-ward.

'As you are, Commander,' said the man. 'And I should not toy with you.' His voice changed, the smile disappeared, and his eyes blazed with something like exultation. 'John Koenig, I am Raan, a citizen of Zenno. Look at Zenno City.'

He waved, and a dazzling panoramic view of the fantastic city Koenig had seen in the big screen of Main Mission Control unfolded and engulfed him. Its rearing towers climbed majestically into a violent purple sky. He was forced backwards. He felt dwarfed, a savage from the jungles of Earth suddenly adrift in a modern city complex.

'You will adjust, John Koenig,' said Raan. 'But first you must know that I read your thoughts. And I understand your feelings of inadequacy. They are well based. It will be thousands of years before your race begins to be able to reach out to us and meet us on something like level terms.'

Koenig looked past the man. Purple was the predominant hue of Zenno. Purple sky, a violent purple sun that hung darkly over the shimmering city. Then Koenig looked back at the man who called himself Raan. *Telepathic.*

Raan nodded.

'Try to adjust, Commander. It's true. I read your mind. And I brought you here.'

'And what of my ship?' Koenig said bitterly. 'And my command?'

'Look.'

Raan's strange eyes shimmered, and the purple sky-city dissolved into a glaring purple void. Koenig again had the sensation of immense distance. And then he saw himself.

He was looking down at the slow-breathing body of John Koenig as if he were one of the half-dozen people in the cabin of the wrecked Eagle. Carter was there, crowded by a pair of medical attendants. Bergman watched the unconscious body—watched *him!* —with a puzzled air of uncomprehending pity. And on Helena Russell's beautiful face was the intent stare of a professional confronted by the inexplicable.

Koenig tensed as he saw the wound on his own forehead. It had been cleaned up, but the gash told of the gravity of the injury.

Helena Russell spoke crisply:

'I can't do anything for him here. He can be moved, Paul.'

Koenig glimpsed Paul Morrow's worried features in the small screen. 'I'll send a Cargo Eagle, Dr Russell. Any reaction, anything at all?'

Koenig watched, fascinated, as Helena ran a finger over his white face. No one else saw the action. She didn't look like a surgeon.

'None,' she said to the screen.

Koenig refused to believe what he saw.

'Hallucination,' said Koenig across the light-years. 'I don't know how I project you, but I'm still on a rock, out of control and lost. You're an unreality.'

Raan waved a hand, and the brilliant purple sky-city formed.

'I understand your incredulity, Commander John Koenig. I won't attempt any further explanation, not yet, but you should know that you have been brought here for a purpose. Think of this, though, whilst you rest and eat. Why did your ship Eagle One search in that particular area?'

Koenig wondered whether he should answer. Answer the projections of one's own mind? If he did that, then he became part of his own fantasy. If he didn't answer, then—he paused—then how did he get to know the answer to the question?

'Well?' he heard himself say.

'We interested you in the possibility of fuel materials, Commander. I had your deductive machines send you there. I wished to isolate you, Commander, put you in a stress situation.'

'And risk killing me?'

Raan smiled, not pleasantly.

'There was little risk. And here you are.'

Koenig looked down at his wrist.

The monitor was blank. Defunct. Life-functions at cessation level, as the computer put it.

'Am I?' he asked.

'Let my daughter convince you,' said Raan.

Koenig felt his emotions somersaulting when he saw her. It was the woman who had appeared momentarily and with such a stunning beauty at Main Mission Control. Her willowy body rippled under the red-gold gown, and her sheaf of pale hair swept her shoulders.

'Your daughter!' said Koenig. They could have been brother and sister. Both were at the age when the ease and strength of maturity replaces youth.

'Tell Commander John Koenig something of life on Zenno, my dear. It will come easier from you. Yes, this is Vana, my daughter.'

The woman smiled.

'Come, John Koenig. Let me show you to your quarters. There is food ready. Everything as you would wish. And trust me—I, too, am real.'

Koenig watched the man called Raan fade into a shimmering purple void. He hung, insubstantially, as the honey-bronze woman had done at Main Mission Control, then he was gone.

'John?' said Vana

Koenig followed. A floor swimming with mosaics led to a hazy glowing shape; as Koenig walked, the shape took on solidity. And then it was a replica of his own quarters on Alpha, the furnishings an exact match for his comfortable private room. The table was laid for one. Koenig disliked eating alone, but the smell of prime steak cooking brought a wash of saliva to his mouth.

Koenig realized that Vana was looking at him as he might have regarded a novel species: with curiosity and amusement.

Koenig felt anger. He controlled it. One should not be afraid of one's own illusions. Yet he had to respond to Vana's half-smile.

'How do you do it?' he asked. He pointed to the

table, the console of the food supply unit, the banks of music selectors, and the rows of well-handled books that had accompanied him from Earth. 'You've got it right, down to my toothbrush.'

'You still think you're hallucinating, don't you, John Koenig? I know. Raan told you that we could see into your mind. We have advanced far beyond your civilization, John. We gave up machines a million years ago. We abandoned intergalactic travel once we had explored where we wished. Our thoughts control the physical things around us—we create and change our lives to suit our moods. Zenno is insubstantial. It is the combined product of our wishes, John. And what you see around you—your living quarters —they *are* a projection, but they are real too. You see, there is a reality which you cannot yet conjecture, John.' She paused and moved closer. 'Did you imagine *me*?'

Koenig looked down into yellow-gold eyes.

'No,' he said slowly. 'The rest, but not you.'

'And you trust me?'

She was very close now. Koenig thought, bewildered, the senses could betray one: her movement, the sheen of honey-gold skin, the bright shimmering material, the wide tawny eyes, and the soft voice. All made their separate and stunning impact. He reached towards her in a timeless moment and saw the response.

'Good!' said an authoritative voice. 'Excellent, Vana—I knew you would be able to convince our friend that we are as real as he is. Well, John Koenig, what is your opinion of Zenno now? Do we exist?'

Koenig made up his mind.

'Tell me what has happened to my command and I'll be able to let you know.'

Raan smiled. 'As I hoped, John Koenig. Loyalty to the group is obviously one of your civilization's motivating forces. Vana, will you reassure the Commander?'

Koenig saw the gladness go from her eyes. 'Of course, Raan. John, please look at your communication screen.'

Koenig turned as the screen filled with life. It showed the interior of the crashed Eagle. Helena Russell was speaking:

'There's a fracture, Paul, but we can hold the loss of blood. I've stabilized that. How about the life-reading?'

'Negative,' said Paul Morrow.

Koenig saw his own inert body encased in a casualty pack. Helena Russell was the calm professional again. The momentary tenderness was quite gone.

'Who is she?' asked Vana.

'A colleague,' said Koenig. 'A friend.'

'A lover?'

Koenig smiled. 'Read my mind.'

Raan looked curiously at Vana. Koenig caught the small frown of puzzlement. It cleared.

'Well, Commander John Koenig? Are you ready to tell us that you believe we exist?'

Koenig knew with an overwhelming certainty that he had been transported on to a far and utterly sophisticated planet.

'It makes no sense at all if you were my own fantasy. Zenno exists,' he said. 'But why should you interest yourself in me?'

'Vana should have explained,' said Raan.

'My father is Zenno's leading anthropologist—' she began, conscious of her lapse.

Raan held up his hand.

'No, my dear. I think the Commander would like to hear it from me.' Koenig saw the man's subdued excitement. 'On Earth, you study the last of your savages, Commander. I know from you that there

are still remote communities which you protect from
the effects of your civilization. You protect them,
because they remind you of your primitive past. They
are your link with your origins.' Raan laughed. 'And
even *they* get some satisfaction from observing the
behaviour of still more primitive forms of life.'

Koenig had a sudden memory of a film he had
seen: a pygmy watching a baboon in a rain-forest
glade.

'Yes, Commander! Exactly. Their link with the
primeval past!'

The laughter was sustained and harsh. Koenig,
listening, suddenly knew his role. Vana was staring
at him, her yellow-gold eyes glistening.

'Raan—' she said in alarm.

'No! John Koenig must be told! Commander, do
you know what you are? I see you do! Why have
we brought you here? You know! You see now that
you are *our* missing link!'

CHAPTER FOUR

'You've been unconscious for two days, John,' said
Victor Bergman.

Koenig opened his eyes fully and recognized the
bleak walls and the diffused lighting. He had been
too many times in the Diagnostic Unit at Medical
Centre to mistake it. Too many lives had slipped
away; too many good men and women lost in the
unending struggle for survival on the harsh rock.

'Victor!' Koenig remembered. 'I was hallucinating—but, good God, it was so, so intense!' He looked around and caught the movement of an orderly, a woman dressed in the white of the Medical teams, slim and sweet-looking, but not a Vana, all honey-bronze under the shimmering gown. Bergman said:

'We've been worried about you, John. How's the head?'

Koenig pushed aside the memories.

'The others—and yourself, Victor?'

Bergman shrugged. 'A couple of ribs cracked. They'll mend. But Sandra Benes is dead, John.'

'Dead!'

'Helena tried. But Sandra seemed to give up.'

'But she wasn't badly hurt!'

'She saw her death and accepted it.'

Koenig pushed down the all-too-familiar angry grief. Bergman must be suffering from the shock of the technician's death. 'We have to take casualities, Victor.'

'Yes!' There was an odd certainty in Bergman's tone of voice and a strange glitter in his eyes. 'More and more casualties, John—don't you see, we've no way of avoiding becoming casualties ourselves! The personnel of Moonbase Alpha isn't limitless. The more that die, the more strain and responsibility it throws on the rest of us. The work doesn't lessen though we do! Eventually, there won't be enough of us to operate Alpha.' He was breathing fast now. 'John, would you like to be the last man alive on this useless chunk of rock? I wouldn't! I'd like to be free of it! John, you and I can't sacrifice ourselves to the rest!'

Koenig was aware of a tenseness in himself now. Bergman was unnaturally excited. The ascetic features were flushed, the aquiline nose seemed hooked and predatory.

'Victor, you sure you've got over the crash?' he said carefully. 'Did Helena give you a final check?'

'Why play big man now!' snarled Bergman. 'We could be live cowards if we took the only correct choice! There's the possibility of escape for a few of us, Koenig. Life's waiting for us out there. Stop worrying about—'

Koenig leaned forward and grabbed the thin, hard shoulder:

'Hold it, Victor!'

He paused, unsure of himself now that he had stopped the tirade. There should be pain. Pain from the head injury. And sorrow for Sandra Benes. But he felt nothing. Only the absence of emotion.

'You're not well,' he told Bergman. 'You're in shock.'

'In shock?' snarled Bergman. 'Me?' He grabbed Koenig's arm. 'Come and see what we found at the scene of the crash!'

Koenig pulled away. Bergman was acting out of character.

His normally articulate speech was more that of a lower-deck Controller accustomed to giving terse orders. There was a hectic excitement about him that belied his ordered, logical mind. Nevertheless, Koenig was impressed by his enthusiasm, however uncharacteristic it might be.

'It's your party, Victor,' he said. 'But no one's mentioned any discovery at the crater.'

'On my instructions!' said Bergman. 'John, it's too important to spread—I ordered a total security clampdown.'

Koenig was unpleasantly affected by the scientist's enthusiasm.

'Well, Victor, what *is* it? Mineral deposits—something we can use as fissile materials?'

'No—there were never any natural deposits in that area! Our computer misread the indications.'

'Misread them? Then what should the computer have suggested?'

'Not here,' said Bergman. 'I'll tell you in your office—and make sure the intercoms are dead. This is just for you, John!'

'It's so important?'

'I told you there was a way out for us!'

Koenig checked the intercom on his wrist. Despite his dislike of secrecy, he made sure that no electronic scribe could relay or record their conversation.

'I think you'd better explain, Victor,' he said.

Bergman would not sit down. Restlessly, he paced about the room for a few seconds. Then he burst out:

'There is good reason for the computer's read-out—it's fissile material all right, John. But the computer didn't take into account one alternative possibility.'

'Well?'

'That the fissile material came from the power unit of another space-craft!'

'What!'

"It's out there, John, under guard—it deceived the computer and it drew our Eagle to the crater!'

Koenig felt a chill spread slowly along his spine.

'You're telling me that there's a space-craft on the Moon?'

'Yes!'

'And it's not one of ours?'

'It's no surface-hopper—John, it's a deep-space vessel! It's got a drive that makes our big burners look like toys. I'd guess it's already covered thousands of light-years.'

'And it showed up as a computer read-out for a load of radioactive metals!'

'That's what it is, so far as the computer is concerned!'

'But if there was life aboard it, the computer would have given us a reading!'

Bergman smiled grimly, 'You're right, John.'

Koenig let the implication of Bergman's information filter through his mind. It brought a fresh chill along his spine. 'So any occupants that might have travelled in it—'

'—are dust. Little heaps of dust.'

Koenig thought of the loneliness they had all endured. And now to be told that there was an alien craft on the Moon!

'How much have you seen?' he asked Bergman.

'Enough to know that they were a species similar to our own. And a whole era of technology in advance of us.'

'And they're dead?'

'Dead for well over a thousand years.'

'And their ship's been here all the time?'

'It's been here since the last days of the Roman Empire.'

Koenig questioned himself. It was too much to hope for. Nevertheless, he said:

'A superior ship to our craft, you say, Victor?'

Bergman answered the unspoken question, and Koenig knew the reason for the secrecy he had insisted on.

'Far better. And in good order.'

'And it landed here—why?'

'You should know that its destination wasn't the moon, John. That was only a stopover.'

'Yes?'

'They would watch, from the satellite. From the Moon, they'd watch Earth. That was the intention, anyway.'

'And then?'

'Their computer would check the life-forms. And if they were able to blend in with us—with our ancestors of the Dark Ages—they would make the final flight.'

'To Earth?'

'Yes, John.' Bergman went on calmly enough, but with a yearning that was painful to see: 'And both engine and computer were in perfect working order. Both waiting for the orders that never came.'

'The final flight. They never gave it?'

'No. And the ship can take us back to Earth!'

CHAPTER FIVE

'That's the ship,' said Bergman.

Koenig was disappointed. The craft was no larger than one of the Eagles. Stubby, scarred by radiation, it lay half-buried under a fall of ash. A port was open.

'The metals are very dense,' said Bergman. 'I'm not familiar with the composition of the materials for the drive—they've confused the computer, of course. I had some analyses run, but they're not enough yet. I had to feed the stuff in manually, John. I don't want any of the technicians to spread the word.'

Koenig marvelled. The ship blended into the background. It was impossible to see it when he stood back a few metres. It was no wonder that the survey-ships had missed it.

'I had new gravity and atmosphere units sent out,' said Bergman.

'You've been busy.'

There was something wrong, though Koenig could not pinpoint why he should feel uneasy. Bergman was right to keep a thing like this to himself. But should he talk so possessively of the ship? And how was it that he had discovered it?

Bergman was ahead of him.

'I stumbled out after the crash—dazed, you know, John. Carter was busy calling Alpha, and you and Sandra Benes were both unconscious. I panicked, I suppose, and ran out. I fell from that ledge and landed against the ship.' He indicated the post. 'I was too dazed to care much about scientific investigation. I must have activated an external switch. It opened at once.'

'So you set up a guard?'

'Yes. With orders not to approach nearer than a hundred metres. I said it was the wreck of an experimental unit I had been testing.'

'So only you know about it—'

'And you, John. Just you and me.'

Koenig felt a prickling around his scalp. Things were taking shape, but still there were inconsistencies.

'What's the trouble, John?' asked Bergman.

'My head.'

'Is it hurting still?'

'It should. But it isn't.'

'I expect Dr Russell made a good job of it.'

'I was badly hurt—'

'You heal quickly.' Bergman indicated the open port. 'See what you make of the ship.'

Koenig forgot his worries. A thousand-year-old mystery lay before him. He clambered through the tilted port and found himself in a brightly-lit command room. Metals glinted, unstained by time. Dials gleamed, and there was the slight pulse that tells a spaceman a ship is alive.

'The crew?' he said.

'Look.'

Koenig turned. A wall of black glass-like material faced him. Behind it, three recesses. Each was slightly more than two metres in height. Each was large enough to hold a man of rather more than average size. Koenig shivered. The long-dead crew of the alien ship had once used those containers. It was as Bergman said. A small heap of dust lay at the bottom of each shadowy recess.

'John, this ship is programmed for a flight to Earth. I've checked its power reserves. It will take three of us back to Earth from any part of the Galaxy.'

'It didn't take them,' said Koenig. The containers were coffins.

'I've checked that too. Their screens must have failed momentarily. There's a tiny hole in the deep-freeze compartment—'

'Deep-freeze?'

'A voyage such as theirs took time. A lot of time. They should have been in suspended animation until their ship was somewhere near the Moon. Long before they reached it, a particle no bigger than a pin-head ruptured their life-support systems.'

'And?'

'They did not regain consciousness.'

'Thank God for that.'

Koenig thought of the three unknown aliens, gently sliding from life to death without waking. The other thing would have been worse—incarcerated, conscious, behind the black material which was far tougher than glass. Waiting for death. But no, they had gradually become dust as the Moon circled the Earth.

'Forget them!' Bergman said violently. 'It's an op-

portunity that will never come again, Koenig—I can
have this ship operational in hours!'

Koenig's head still felt muzzy, his thoughts
unclear.

'Operational?'

'Koenig, you're not thinking, man! It's our chance!
We take the ship! Any three Alphans can be on a
course for Earth within the next few hours. I've
looked at the life-support systems. Whoever the aliens
were, they had the same kind of metabolism as ours.
They needed more oxygen and a trace of a couple of
ple of gases we don't use, but I can have the tanks
converted with no trouble. Look, Koenig, call David
Kano and have him bring some equipment. Swear
him to secrecy, first. Call him, John!'

'Kano you mean, offer him a place?'

'Yes! You, me, and Kano!'

Koenig had the sense of wrongness that had troubled
him during the short Eagle trip to the crater. Bergman's
excitement, his own inability to reason: there was
more. He looked beyond the crater's rim, thinking
of the dust settling on the ancient vessel. Then he
saw the purple-tinged star. His head hurt and he looked
down.

'Bergman,' he said, 'what gives you the right to
choose who stays and who goes?'

'Finding the ship! It's the law of possession, John!'

'So we leave. You, our best brain. David Kano,
our top technician. And me.'

'What are we leaving? A barren rock on a flight
to nowhere!'

'And what of the others? What about Helena Russell?'

'Then let her come! But get Kano to ensure the
life-support systems are checked! And be careful how
you make the request, John. If word gets out, we'll

have a full-scale mutiny on our hands. Let's get this ship away as soon as we can!'

Koenig closed his eyes. The green fields were very close now. Blue skies, the sound of leaves, the feel of rain on his face. He thought of a girl he had known, pale-skinned, who had swum like a mermaid in a warm Cretan sea one golden summer. He could go back.

And then he had a distant memory of a walk back to Moonbase Alpha. A walk of a hundred miles. Black rock, dust, jagged horizons. It had taken such a short time. He looked up again, sensing constraint as he did so: he saw the star-system edged in purple.

'That star-system,' he said to Bergman.

'Which?'

'There.'

Bergman ignored the question:

'Look, John, if it will satisfy you, I'll ask the computer to give a reading as to who's eligible for the third place in the ship. What do you say?'

Koenig thought it reasonable. But the star-system persisted in drifting before him. Bergman was impatient.

'Call Kano!' he ordered.

'Leave them behind?' Koenig said slowly, for the first time fully appreciating what Bergman proposed. 'Leave them to face *that*?'

And he raised his hand to the emptiness beyond the strange star-system.

'Leave them? Yes! And be damned to them! What have they ever done for you? Or for themselves? You've had to make every decision for them! Don't think that they'll be any safer if you stay, John! The Alphans are finished—save yourself!'

Koenig looked at his heavy gauntleted fist. Anger flooded through him. Rage shook his tall, muscular frame. Bergman flinched as the mailed fist began to swing towards his visor.

And Koenig stopped it.

The blow never fell. Instead, Koenig's mind blazed with a new fury. And then he lunged free of the Moon's weak gravity, disregarding Bergman's now frenzied pleas. A wild purple void rushed towards him.

'Raan!' yelled Koenig. 'Raan!'

The crater, the alien ship, the Moon itself fell away in purple shadows and Bergman too merged with the void. Koenig tried to peer into the blazing purple haze.

'Raan!' he yelled. 'I'm not an animal! I'm a man!'

Walls slowly materialized about him. The void gave way to the quarters which should be his but were a projection of the Zennite's mind. Koenig tensed, expecting Raan to appear. Instead Vana came to him.

'John?', she called. 'My father doesn't mean to harm you!' Koenig knew that he had been used. He felt defiled.

'He's using me as a laboratory animal! It wasn't Bergman I saw—just another of your Zennite tricks! There never was an alien ship! It was all a fake! And so is this!'

Koenig included the living quarters in his wide sweep.

Vana's face registered shock.

'But he is a scientist, John—no more and no less. He would never inflict pain or degradation on you. He seeks only the truth about you.'

Koenig stared at her for a few moments. She could read his mind; but what if she were incapable of understanding the thoughts that filled it?

Slowly his fury subsided.

'Vana,' he said. 'Understand this. Your father is

setting up situations to test my reactions. It wasn't Bergman I talked to and Sandra Benes didn't die. It was a deliberately invented stress situation.'

'You were clever to guess it.'

'No. I know Bergman would never consider abandoning the Alphans. No more than I could. Your experiment failed, Raan.'

Vana stepped closer, and Koenig caught the delicate scent. He was looking into the gold-flecked eyes once more. A new emotion replaced his anger.

'Again you surprise me, John Koenig,' he heard.

Vana and he looked at Raan.

'I think, John Koenig, that you might well have attempted violence if Vana had not spoken to you first. I find the prospect fascinating!' His handsome face was alive with enthusiasm. 'Vana is right, Commander—I have no wish to humiliate you, but how can I observe your reactions if there is no stress situation? Commander, what I and my colleagues see is something that has been absent from our culture for a million years! In you we can see in action the blind furies that before were only text-book abstractions to us. Murder, war, torture—they are present in your thought, even if suppressed. Those, your admirable group-loyalty, and your amazing intuitive insight into your companions—that is what we study, Commander! But why did the experiment fail?'

Koenig said:

'You got the technology right, I'll give you that. I believed that such a ship as you projected could make Earth. It was logical that an alien would inspect Earth from the Moon, and it was within the limits of probability that their ship would be holed. But you don't know *men!* All right, you've gained two million years on Earthmen, but have you *really* changed, Raan? I doubt it. Tell me, have you faced any threat to your existence in all that time—as a group, as a race?'

'No, John Koenig,' said Raan. 'No.'

'When you are threatened, do you think you will be unemotional?'

Raan did not answer for some time.

'I don't know, John Koenig. Perhaps that was the purpose of the experiment: to find out about the Zennite psyche.'

'And when you've finished your investigation, what then? Will you send me back to Alpha?'

Raan looked at Vana. She reached out a hand to Koenig.

'John, you can't return. It is no longer possible.'

Koenig looked from the tall handsome man to the slim, elegant girl with the beautiful eyes.

'Is this another experiment?' he said harshly.

'No, John,' said Vana. 'See.'

Koenig gripped the hand until the purple void closed in again. Time and space altered subtly, and the sensation of huge distances, mind-reeling leaps across the gulfs had him by the throat. He heard the Zennite woman say: 'You are dying, John.'

He was watching Paul Morrow struggle with indecision. The big screen in Main Mission Control filled with light and then settled. Koenig could see Helena Russell, and beyond her his own long frame.

'What are the chances, Dr Russell?' said Morrow.

Helena Russell pushed her long blonde hair back from her face wearily. 'The fracture can be treated. The rest is superficial. But how can I give a medical opinion about *that?*'

She pointed to the registers that showed no life-activity.

'I'll try revival procedures.'

She indicated to the assistants what she required.

'What's Professor Bergman's opinion now?' asked Morrow.

'What it has been from the first,' Bergman said. He approached the scarce-breathing body. 'We're faced with a paradox. John Koenig is neither dead nor alive. Apparently there has been a cessation of electrical activity throughout the nerve centres. Yet he breathes. It's so unnatural as to be unbelievable. I am convinced that he is affected by some external agency which we can't investigate because our computer can't begin to define it.' He looked down at the glittering electrodes on the shaven head. 'If I were a superstitious man, I'd say that his soul had been stolen.'

'That's nonsensical—' Morrow snapped angrily, but Helena Russell was already speaking. Morrow stopped to listen.

'I'm reinforcing the charge by two more electrodes over the heart, Victor. No, I'll do it,' she told her assistant. When they were in place, she looked up at the screen. 'Victor isn't being fanciful,' she said. 'If it's a spell, we'll break it.'

'Or John,' said Morrow. His voice was loud in Main Mission Control. 'I can't authorize this, Dr Russell! It's the crudest kind of treatment! Damn it, Helena, shock therapy is an archaic and discredited form of treatment! You've even said yourself there's an odds-on chance you'll kill him! And I won't permit it! I'm in command now and I say—'

Kano snarled: 'You say nothing, Morrow! If there's any decision to be made, Dr Russell will make it! You're not the Commander of Moonbase Alpha any more than I am!'

Morrow swung round furiously. He was faced with something he could not understand. Outright opposition could be dealt with, whereas the eerie thing that had happened to John Koenig left him dismayed and helpless. His fists balled.

Appalled, John Koenig turned to Vana. 'They're falling apart,' he said slowly. 'It's going to wreck Moonbase.'

Instinctively he ordered Morrow to calm down, but Morrow couldn't hear. Koenig realized that his presence at Moonbase was only a projection sent across the continuums to watch his own death. Gritting back the angry words, Koenig heard Helena Russell say:

'I made this decision, Controller Morrow.'

Paul Morrow's anger ebbed. Helena Russell nodded to her assistant. 'Half-power,' she said.

There was dead silence in the Diagnostic Unit. Then Koenig saw his own shaven head jerk once, twice, as the power surged through his inert body. A sympathetic shudder raced along his spine. Vana clutched his hand.

'Well?' said Paul Morrow.

Helena Russell's blue eyes were fixed on the life-line readings. Momentarily the red electronic lines began to creep upwards.

'Raise it three points,' she said.

'He can't stand that charge!' Kano called.

'I can't leave him like this. He's dead, a zombie!' Helena said bitterly.

The assistant hesitated, then looked at Morrow.

'Raise the level,' said the Controller.

Koenig saw the shaven head jerk again. Then it slumped back, eyes open and unseeing.

Vana wept, and then Koenig sensed the power she began to exert. Space bent. Light-years flashed past. The Diagnostic Unit faded and merged into a rushing, purple void. There was an echo of Helena

Russell's low sigh, and then Koenig saw the strange towers of Zenno form about him.

Raan was there, subdued and watching them with a worried expression:

'Well, John Koenig? What do you see as your future now? Can you make the adjustment? Are you strong enough to come out of the jungle and cross into the city? Can you become a Zennite?'

Koenig held Vana for a moment, then he gently pushed her aside. It was she who spoke for him:

'Haven't you seen enough, Father? Do you have to watch him suffer like this? Can't you see that John can never have the kind of intellectual detachment you have? He is not a man of our times, Father! He may be a primitive, but he is still a man—perhaps even a better man than you! We have no right to tear him away from his people and use him as a testing ground!'

Raan's hard gaze bored into Koenig. Koenig looked back, steadily aware of the probing, fierce intelligence that drilled into his mind. Raan's puzzlement was obvious.

'I find this difficult to believe, Commander,' he said. 'I can no longer read your mind. I have an impression of unrest and a decision impending, but I cannot come to any conclusion about your intentions. He turned to Vana. 'And your thoughts, too, are hidden from me.' He laughed. 'It is almost as though you, John Koenig, and you too, Vana, are subject to strong and almost—primitive—emotion!'

He watched for a while. And then the purple haze hid him. Koenig felt Vana's slim softness, very close.

'I've read of it in the ancient texts,' she said. 'I don't suppose any of our people have ever experienced it.' Vana smiled. 'John, isn't it called "love"?'

CHAPTER SIX

Koenig knew what it was like to be young again. The hours passed in a slow and dazzling procession, each minute bringing its own excitement. Vana was by his side as he explored Zenno.

'John, see—we project our image of the city, and when we find a new way of expressing ourselves, we can alter it. You will learn, John! You have the intelligence, and you can develop the skills.'

It seemed to Koenig that he was drifting in a web of purple haze. Force-fields bore him up above the city and its glorious towers. Below, he could see Zennites casually wandering amongst flowered terraces, all young and strong. Sometimes one or another would drift away from a group, to soar through the purple night on his own inspired errand.

'It's a world of dreams,' said Koenig. 'It has the texture of reality, but it's so tenuous! It changes so quickly—shape, colour, quality! I see it, and then I can't take in the shapes—I can't imagine how I could begin to form anything so beautiful.'

'But you'll have time, John! Time, and the best instructors! We don't live your brief span of years, John! Why, my father has lived for over five centuries in your terms, and he is still a young man. We have a dozen of your lifetimes ahead of us. And the stars, too! We can show you how to sail out far beyond any galaxy you knew—we can take you into parts of the Universe where life is still being created. Only say you'll stay here on Zenno, and my father and I can stop trying to support that part of you which belongs to your planet. Say it, John!'

Koenig felt the woman's surge of love. It washed through and over him with a warmth he had not known since the first glow of emergent manhood. There had been women, and not a few either; Koenig had accepted life as it came to him. But nothing, no one, had stirred him as Vana did now.

'I have to believe you,' he said. 'I have to believe that this is true. I know that I have your love, and I hope you do not doubt mine, Vana.' His hand came up to his forehead. 'When I think that I am here because of your father's experiment, I find it ironic. You, Vana, in love with what to him is an ape-man.'

Vana threw himself around him.

'Ape-man, Earthman, space-man, star-man! You'll stay—I know it!'

Koenig held her close.

'How could I leave you?'

Raan was waiting when they returned to the brilliant apartment which Vana had summoned into being. Already, Koenig could begin to understand how a human mind could master the subtleties of the inner dimensions. The Zennites had advanced their minds, but they were humans. What they could do, so might he. Raan looked sombrely at them.

'So you have made your decision, Commander?'

Koenig was immediately alert. He might be two million years behind in intellect, but he knew when a man put out a challenge.

'I've decided,' he said. 'I stay here, on Zenno.'

'You surprise me, Commander.'

'Why, Father?' said Vana. 'Is there any reason why John should not stay?'

'He must judge for himself, Vana.'

'But you've told me that you can't sustain my life on Alpha—how can there be any choice?' demanded Koenig. Raan's cold grey eyes were full of an unreadable calculation. Not dislike, not challenge, thought Koenig. There was almost a look of pity there. And why pity *now?*

Koenig felt a cold, uneasy sensation, ghosts plucked at the fringes of his mind. The Zennite purple was heavy, black-edged, suddenly menacing.

Raan's gaze cleared, as if he had solved his calculation.

'Now I read your mind again, John Koenig,' said Raan. 'I know there is love for my daughter.' He smiled sadly. 'I have read of this emotion. You have the symptoms, and Vana too. It clouds your judgement.'

'You'd better say what you mean,' said Koenig in a level voice, with a coldness at his heart.

'No!' called Vana. 'I know!'

She glared at her father.

'You want to take him back to that condemned base! You want him to waste his life on a bleak rock amongst those primitives. But he won't! John, I'll break the hold we have on you—I'll release you from the constricting brief life. I need you more than they. John, you'll be the finest of the Zennites!'

When she stopped, Koenig said, 'Well, Raan?'

'I can keep the link for a little longer. Long enough for you to judge for yourself, John Koenig. And then you can tell me about the power of love.'

Koenig braced himself as the Zennite harnessed the forces of his incredible intellect. He heard Vana call out, and then the mind-reeling purple void took him in its grip.

Time hung still as the vivid haze formed. Space rushed away in a colossal tide. And then, about him, the bleak contours of Moonbase Alpha began to form.

Koenig saw at once that a crisis had developed.

He hurried through the long corridors. There was no echo as his shoes hit the floor. A hurrying technician would have walked into him had Koenig not sprung aside. Koenig realized that he was only a projection, a thing without substance. No one could see him. He was still a captive of the Zennite's fantastic trickery. But why send him back? Why now, after he had seemed to be accepted on Zenno?

He made for Main Mission Control and saw why.

A technician was struggling in the grip of a red-faced security guard. Another of the big purple-uniformed men ran to help.

'Watch him!' bawled Paul Morrow. 'He had a gun!'

Koenig ran. No one noticed him.

Kano bent to pick up the black-handled weapon which had slid from the technician's paralysed hand.

'Put it down!' Morrow ordered.

Kano looked at Paul Morrow in incredulous amazement.

'No one handles weapons except Security!' Morrow snapped. 'And that includes you, Kano!'

'You didn't think I—'

'He's one of your men isn't he?' snapped Morrow. 'How do I know who's in this madness? First the fist-fights, then this—bring him here!' he ordered.

'It's Devereaux, sir,' said the security guard. 'First-class Technician.'

'How did you get the gun?' said Morrow.

Deveraux's lips were badly cut. Blood dripped down his jacket. 'I'm saying nothing.'

Morrow's big hands bunched.

'Then tell me why you're here—what do you want,

man! Don't you know that this craziness is wrecking Alpha? What's got into you?'

Devereaux was not a young man. His slight body seemed too weak for the fight he had put up. Now, his will cracked. Defeated, he said:

'We know Commander Koenig isn't dead. And what you want to do! It isn't any good, Controller! We heard Commander Koenig could be saved. He'd have a chance if you left him on the machines—but you've given the order to disconnect them!'

Morrow turned to Kano,

'Who started that rumour? Someone did! Sergeant,' he said to the security guard, 'take Devereaux away and find out where it began! And report any similar incidents!'

The big screen on the forward con jangled an electronic warning.

'This is Johnson, Security,' said a hard-faced guard. 'Trouble in the Diagnostic Unit, sir! I'm keeping a bunch of crewmen out—they've heard the rumour too!'

He turned away, and the screen filled with flying bodies. A nurse screamed, and a tray of instruments crashed on to the floor. Koenig did not stay to hear more.

'I've seen enough. Vana, get me out of here,' he called. 'Raan! RAAN!'

Moonbase Alpha was falling apart. After all, he was the pivot on which so many lives balanced. In any normal situation, no man was indispensable. By the nature of social organization, another leader should have emerged to take over. But the Alphans were not in a normal situation. Extended by the demands of keeping alive, living through crises almost daily, they identified one man with survival—John Koenig.

Helena Russell had told him as much, and he had

denied it. But it was true. Until the overwrought Alphans could adjust to the harshness of their lives, they would pin their hopes, project their fears, on him.

'Raan!' he yelled, desperately.

Raan and Vana plucked him through the shouts of the Alphans, guided him amongst the eerie purple shades, and waited until his disrupted nerves had settled.

Vana was weeping.

'I read your mind now, John Koenig,' said Raan. 'Will you believe me when I say I am sorry?'

Koenig took a step towards Vana. Her splendid gold-flecked eyes swam with misery. He reached out and ran a hand down her cheek. The skin was warm and vital. Koenig looked beyond her. Zenno had changed subtly. The towers were rounded, softer now. With a desperate longing Koenig had a moment of insight into the ways in which it was possible to structure such shapes. An Earthman could learn.

'Stay, John!' whispered Vana.

'I can't. However much I want to. You saw what was happening at Alpha. Your father is right—we are a primitive society still, with the shortcomings and the superstitions of the tribe. We haven't yet learned to dispense with emotion, and our emotions can still wreck us.' He sighed. 'I can no more stay here than you, Vana, could come back with me to Alpha.'

"I'll come!"

'No. It would be the worst kind of imprisonment for you, Vana. However much we meant to each other, the day would soon come when your mind ranged out into regions where our narrow intellects could not follow, and you would be alone. I am bound to my people, you must not be.'

Raan detached Vana's hand from Koenig's arm.

'I brought you here as an experiment, John Koenig,' he said. 'I have learned more than I dared hope. You awakened in Vana's heart something that I thought dead in the souls of the Zennites—and perhaps more of us might rediscover what we have lost.' He looked past Koenig, and the Alphan saw in the keen stare something like awe. 'I think we could respond to danger, John Koenig. And I hope we would have your courage when it came.'

He shivered with concentration, staring into the brilliant purple void. 'You must hurry!' he said. 'My power to hold you at such a distance is failing. Go now, John Koenig, and remember Zenno!'

'And think of me, John?' whispered Vana. 'In the days when you see a new star-system for the first time, think of me?'

Koenig's self-control was at an end. He pulled the woman to him:

'Think of me too, Vana!'

'Go!' she whispered fiercely. 'Go, before I let that other Koenig slip away and keep you here forever!'

Raan's eyes blazed. The purple void began to shadow Koenig's mind. Through it, he saw the slim body of the woman he loved. The last he saw of her was her hand, raised in a hopeless gesture of farewell.

Orderlies were still clearing up the shattered instruments and containers. Dr Russell's hands paused over the controls.

'I think he's gone,' she said. 'You're right, Paul. We're keeping a shell functioning. John Koenig is dead.'

'I can't believe it,' said Bergman. 'Yet we have the evidence before us. Nothing on the screen. No sign of life.'

The recording lines were at zero.

'Yes?' said Helena Russell.

'I take the responsibility,' said Paul Morrow. 'Let him go.'

Helena Russell switched off the life-support system. No delicate pulsor pumped blood through Commander Koenig's veins. No heat-unit stabilized his body-temperature. His chest filled once with air and his mouth showed the slight movement of air sighing out. And then he was still.

The slight mutter of liquids was gone.

'He's gone,' said Kano.

'Then we're finished too,' said Helena Russell.

Only Bergman said nothing. He looked closer. His lips were trembling. A weird purple haze seemed to close about Koenig's head.

'Look!' he said. Look!'

Koenig's eyes opened. His lips moved. Then, unbelievably, the life-lines mounted the recording tubes. Heart, lungs, endocrinal systems registered. The central nervous system showed life.

'But he died!' said an orderly, aghast.

'He's breathing strongly—he's alive!' cried Helena.

Alive!

Throughout the great base the news spread, quicker than any of the grim rumours that had sparked off so much bitterness and violence. The Commander was alive!

Life filled the body.

Koenig focused on Helena Russell's face. He saw the tender concern and wondered why he felt so sad. Then he remembered Vana.

'Welcome back, John,' said Dr Russell. 'We thought we'd lost you—no, don't try to talk! With that split in your head, you need a few weeks of minimal effort. But we'll get you well, John, we're all sure of it!'

Bergman looked down.

'Can you hear me, John?'

Koenig mouthed 'Yes.' The effort was huge, the pain horrific. He knew, without asking, that the wide, deep gash was back.

'Do you know where you've been?'

Koenig thought of the majestically eerie city. And then Vana.

'Yes,' he said in a voice so sad that Bergman was shocked.

'John, I think I can guess at some of it. But I won't. I'll never mention it unless you do first. Is that what you want?'

Koenig breathed *'Yes!'*

Maybe time would dim the image of the gold-flecked eyes, the softly curved body, and the glorious promise of Zenno itself as a background to their love. Maybe the daily routine and the unremitting harshness of life at Alpha would help him forget Vana.

Koenig hoped so. Without really believing it.

'There are one or two things I have to ask you about, John—' began Paul Morrow. He stopped as Dr Russell pushed him aside. "—but not yet. They'll keep. Just as long as you're with us.'

Koenig closed his eyes. *I am,* he thought. *God help me, I'm with you. All the way.*

But the sadness persisted. That, and the ache of loneliness.

CHAPTER SEVEN

The rock that was refuge, prison and space-ship for the Alphans hung poised to cross the great gulf between the island-universes. Koenig watched from his sick-bed. No one could remain unmoved by the sheer immensity of the gulf. No stars. Sable blackness, the end of the galaxy. Koenig knew what every last man and woman at Moonbase Alpha was thinking, there were no star maps now.

Paul Morrow called to him, 'Watching, John? We're leaving the galaxy.'

Koenig said, 'There's a lot of space out there. But we'll make it.'

Morrow caught the tension in his voice. 'How's the head?'

'I don't feel a thing.' He did. The migraine had been identified by Helena Russell. She was using a mixture of drugs and hypnosis to rid him of it. Without success.

'Dr Russell wants to look in.'

'Tell Helena I'm fine. I'll read a book for a while and maybe come up to Main Mission later.'

Paul Morrow nodded and broke the contact.

"How is he?' asked David Kano.

'You heard. The same old John, but hollow inside.' Morrow watched the vast emptiness for a while. 'She must have been some woman.'

'He's told you about her?'

48

'Only that he and she talked. John isn't one to discuss his relationships. But she's left a gap in his life. Everyone knows it.'

'He's recovering,' said Kano. 'I talked to Helena. The fractures healed well, with no permanent damage. She could remove the scar if he'd let her. The headaches have no physical cause. When he forgets the Zennite woman, they'll go.'

'I wish he'd come out.'

'Give him time.'

Morrow looked out again. 'We've had no trouble for weeks. It's just as well. Morale's been good, but the crew want to see him up and around.'

Koenig lay back on his bunk and reached for the battered book of poetry. The book fell open at a couplet he had chanced on:

'All days are nights to see till I see thee
And nights bright days when dreams do
    show me thee.'

Koenig read the lines and felt the thin knife-edge of agony burn into his brain.

Six storeys below Main Mission Control, an alarm buzzed in Technician Anton Zoref's ear. He disregarded it, but his wife shook him:

'Out, Anton—you've time to shave and eat before you go now.'

'Can't they programme us for duty shifts together?' he yawned. 'I hate to leave you in bed, Eva. Husband on duty, you turning over. It's wrong. In any well-run establishment it would be declared immoral.'

He breakfasted quickly and reached his post in the maintenance area of Number Two Nuclear Generator two minutes early. He couldn't know that a moonquake had rocked the foundations of the structure when the Moon was hurled free of Earth's gravitational grasp. In the colossal explosion the small quake had never been recorded.

'Any problems?' he asked Mike Dominix, his opposite number and friend.

'Oh, we had our moment of high drama. Small fuse gone about three a.m. I ok'd the maintenance programme. Eva still asleep?' he grinned.

Zoref slung a shadow-punch at him, fast and hard. Dominix caught it in his big hand.

'See you later, Anton. Don't let the pot boil over!'

It was standard ribaldry of the nuclear generating fraternity. The pot was the sullenly-glowing core of the huge reactor, a frightful hell-brew of white hot metals.

'I'll let you know if it does,' agreed Zoref.

Professor Bergman was the first to spot the pulsing record of energy from the gulf.

'Paul, do you read this?' he called from Main Mission Control. A grey-black blotch showed on the screen.

Paul Morrow was with Koenig trying to get him to take an interest in a modification of the Eagle's navigational aids which had been suggested by a bright young female technician. Koenig had been politely remote. Bergman sounded concerned but not worried.

'I was talking to John,' Morrow said. He hesitated. 'All right, John, I'll leave you in peace. I'll check the sighting with Victor.'

Koenig nodded. 'Let me know if it's important.'

'Controller Morrow!' called a crewman. It was urgent now. 'Professor Bergman indicates a state of alert!'

'On my way!' yelled Morrow.

His place was in Main Mission Control. Koenig

watched him go. The migraine almost blinded him. *An emergency,* he registered. *Not serious. A sighting of an energy-source. What is it?*

He had surprised himself by his own response. For the first time in nearly a month, he had taken an interest in Moonbase Alpha and its headlong dive into deep space.

Then he remembered the woman, and pain began. 'Paul can handle it,' he said. He reached for the tablets which would bring peace.

'What do you think?' asked Morrow tightly.

'It's an energy source,' said Bergman. 'It has to be. Our scanners give it that shape and that strength'— he indicated the grey-black pulsing blotch on the screen—'but computer says it can only approximate the thing.' He turned to Kano. 'What's your view?'

Kano shrugged.

'What the computer can't read, it can't tell us. It's a so-far unobserved form of radiation. And it's altogether too complex in nature for the computer to unscramble. The trouble is, it's changing so rapidly. Almost as if—'

'—as if it were alive,' finished Bergman.

'And it came from *there,*' said Morrow. He pointed towards the deeps of space. They all looked out of the forward con.

'Sighting references eight-zero-beta approaching Moonbase Alpha, range between twenty and twenty-five thousand kilometres,' called a crewman. 'Closing fast.'

Bergman watched the grey-black shape swirling in the electronic haze of the screen. 'Get John!' he called. 'Get the Commander!'

'Commander Koenig to Main Mission Control!' immediately called a crewman. 'Commander to Control!'

'I think we should intercept,' said Bergman.

'With what?' said Morrow.

'Anything we can launch!' Bergman answered. 'It's too fast and too active—can't we stop it?'

'Use main armament?' said Kano. 'The fission bombs? They've never been used offensively, Victor! We'd need authorization—' He stopped himself. He meant to say that only a World Government directive could unleash the fury of the fission bombs. 'We could,' he went on rapidly. There was no government to refer to now.

'Commander Koenig should authorize their use,' Morrow said, responding to the urgency of the two men and his own evaluation of the threatening blotch from the gulf. 'Where is he?'

Koenig was dreaming of purple towers and gold-flecked eyes.

'Sighting reference eight-zero-beta slowing,' said the same crewman. 'Rapid deceleration. Range, eighteen thousand kilometres.'

'Commander Koenig's in a narcotized sleep!' reported another crewman. 'I can't rouse him, Controller!'

Morrow's face showed annoyance and indecision. Then he made up his mind.

'Arm main launchers one to six,' he said. 'I want twelve one-megaton warheads for close-proximity interception.' He noticed Bergman's relief. 'I think you're right Victor. We'll neutralize it.'

'Can't Dr Russell counteract the narcotic?' asked Kano.

'No time,' said Morrow. 'Range?' he snapped to the crewman on the intercept ranger.

'Still constant at eighteen thousand kilometres—no, sir, it's moving again!'

'Main launchers one through six armed!' called

a young ballistics engineer in a voice that quavered with tension. The launchers had never been used. They were part of a deterrent force that had so far justified its name.

'It's changing,' said Bergman.

Confirming his reading of the thing from the gulf, an electronic voice cut in:

'Sighting reference eight-zero-beta now has new structure. Unidentifiable, but with some organic characteristics.' It paused. 'Detailed read-out follows—'

'No details!' said Morrow. 'I want a multiple launch. Box the—the *thing*—with simultaneous detonations. On my word—ready?'

'Ready, Controller,' said the young ballistics engineer.

There was a deep silence in Main Mission Control. Bergman wondered if they were going to blast out of existence an alien life-force. A wonderful thing. Or something of great potential harm.

Morrow opened his mouth to give the order. It never came.

As the electronic circuitry cleared for the impulse that would send the rockets surging from Moonbase Alpha, the big screen cleared.

The grey-black blotch vanished.

'Gone!' breathed Kano. Bergman's voice echoed his: 'No readings!'

Almost in the same instant, the clamour of electronic and human reports filled Main Mission Control.

'Sighting reference eight-zero-beta now had nil readings. Object sighted is not in the range of Moonbase Alpha scanners. Detailed read-out follows!'

'Orders, sir?' asked the young armaments technician.

Morrow realized that his mouth was still open. 'Remain on alert,' he said.

'It's gone,' said Bergman.

'Are we sure?' Morrow asked.

'What the scanners can't sense, we can't reach,' said David Kano. 'But it can't just vanish!'

They looked at the screen. It showed a segment of deep black space. Where the grey-black blotch had writhed like a malignant tumour, there was nothing. Morrow breathed out slowly.

'Launchers on instant readiness,' he said. 'Until my order rescinded. And get Dr Russell up here!'

Zoref had finished the routine checks. He thought he would put forward his projected scheme for random checks. It was his view that the monitors themselves should be stripped at random. That way, the unexpected might be spotted, whereas maintenance at fixed intervals could lead to over-reliance on the machines.

He looked at his watch.

Coffee time. He passed the high, thick wall of the main screen surrounding Nuclear Generator Two, the biggest on Moonbase. And the best-maintained, he thought. As always he could not resist a glance at the writhing coils deep in the heart of the reactor: scanners brought the image, but it was clear and sharp. Since school he had been awed by the temerity of mankind in taming and harnessing the might of nuclear fission; and Eva shared his feelings.

If they hadn't been caught up in the giant nuclear catastrophe that blasted the Moon from his parent body, they would have been doing just the same kind of work. Zoref was one of the few Alphans who didn't much regret their enforced voyage.

He smiled as he switched on the percolator. So much power behind the massive screens and it didn't even keep the coffee warm against the generator.

He was very near the flaw in the skin of Moonbase Alpha now.

'John,' said Helena Russell. She turned his face and dabbed his forehead. He didn't wake up. She opened one eye and saw the pupil at a pinpoint.

'It couldn't disappear,' said Bergman.

'At least it's gone,' pointed out Morrow. 'No alien energy-source has been reported for the past hour.'

'But energy just can't lose itself!' Bergman insisted. 'It must disperse—there has to be *some* reading!' He turned to David Kano. 'Isn't there anything at all from the computer?'

'It's turned sullen,' said Kano. 'It won't admit the thing can vanish. And it won't come up with a theory.'

Bergman frowned. 'I don't have any either. We haven't any information for any kind of hypothesis. David, will you try something for me?'

Kano nodded. 'Of course.'

'See if there's a record *anywhere*—even on one of the smaller sensors or scanners—anywhere in Alpha. Check the manual systems as well.'

'The computer would have checked.'

'But aren't there some systems too minute, too unimportant, for the computer to consider?'

'In theory, no.'

'But it could happen?'

'What's the intention?' asked Morrow.

'It bothers me,' said Bergman. 'We'd have a sighting of the object if it reversed its course and went back into deep space. Similarly, if the energy was dispersed it should show up as a cloud. So it's not gone back into deep space, and it isn't out there,' he said, pointing to the high forward con. 'Where is it?'

'That leaves only one place,' said Kano, paling.

Morrow punched a button.

'Get him awake!' he snapped to Helena Russell.

'I'm trying,' she answered.

'Try harder!'

The hidden flaw bent, buckled, gave way.

Zoref took the first sip, then sent the cup and the scalding liquid flying across the small recess. His yell rang around the great deserted Maintenance Area. Then he pitched forward, throwing a huge shadow over the floor.

He was aware of a swirling grey-blackness and a tearing, bitter cold that anaesthetized his senses even as he lost consciousness.

It said a good deal for his dedication to duty, and also his training, that he managed to hit the panic button. A screaming alarm filled the generating area as he pitched forward.

'Technician Zoref—' he gasped, as the grey-black shadow enveloped him. 'Emergency, Number Two Nuclear Generating Area!'

CHAPTER EIGHT

Commander John Koenig heard the alarm. He moved his head slightly and groaned.

'I didn't want you wakened, John,' said Helena Russell. 'How is it?'

'Bearable. Why the panic?'

Morrow burst into the room.

'John? You'll have to snap out of it—can you make

Main Mission Control on your own feet? I want the crew to see you there, John!'

'What happened?'

'Some kind of emergency in Number Two NGA. But Bergman's worried about the disappearance of an alien energy source. I nearly had it blasted with the main armament, but it vanished before the launch. John?'

'He's still slightly narcotized,' said Helena.

'Get him on his feet!'

'It's too soon!'

'I'll make it,' said Koenig. He dragged on his tunic. 'Get back to Control,' he told Morrow.

Morrow was startled. It was the first direct order he had received since Koenig's accident.

'Yes, sir,' he said hesitantly.

Koenig refused Helena Russell's help.

'It seems I've got a base to run,' he said. The pain had begun again. He tried not to wince. 'No pills,' he told Helena. 'They're getting to be a habit.'

Back in Main Control Koenig rapidly assessed the situation.

'The energy-source we'll worry about later,' he said. 'Do as Professor Bergman recommends. Even the manual monitors—check every possible recording device. And put out a request for any—repeat *any*—unusual occurrence.'

'Where are you going, John?' asked David Kano.

'You're coming too,' said Koenig. 'I want to see this technician.'

Zoref's call had brought his opposite number on the night shift back from his bed. Mike Dominix looked puzzled. The section chief looked frankly incredulous about his story.

'Tell me,' said Koenig. 'You hit the panic-button. You must have had good reason.'

Zoref swallowed. He looked worried.

'There's nothing wrong,' he said. 'No faults, no radiation leaks. I don't remember activating the alarm.'

'It was this circuit,' said the section chief. 'I checked, sir. Zoref was alone here. Right, Dominix?'

Dominix's face was creased with concern.

'It's right, isn't it, Anton?'

'Right,' Zoref said, the word choking him.

'We can't afford chances in this area,' said Kano. 'I'll check it over myself, if you like, Commander.'

'Do that,' said Koenig. The pain was bad. Nothing useful had been accomplished by his intervention. 'Go off duty, Zoref,' he said. 'Maybe you need some rest.'

'But, Commander, I have to look after a lot of maintenance units—'

'You heard the Commander,' said Kano, as Koenig walked away. 'Get a medical check-up before you return to quarters.

Dominix watched his friend walk away. Zoref was one of the steadiest men he had ever met. He frowned. Even Anton could get Alpha-jitters, it seemed. At least it proved he was human.

He watched David Kano working methodically from monitor to monitor. The section chief noted recordings and passed on information to the computer. It was a double check on the automatic maintenance systems. Then Dominix saw Kano stop for several seconds, his small compact body stiff. When he spoke, Kano's voice held a partially-suppressed note of worry:

'Get Professor Bergman,' he said. And: 'Victor— I've found a massive energy discharge down here.'

'A fault in the screens?'

'No. Just a massive energy-loss. Apparently straight from the conversion units. It's recorded by local sensors, but there's been a cut-out so it didn't show on the main circuits.'

'Was Zoref affected?'

'I'll ask Dr Russell.' Both men waited until their communicators hooked into the Diagnostic Unit. 'Dr Russell—have you examined Technician Zoref?' asked Kano.

'I have.'

'And?'

'He's fatigued, unusually so. There's some difficulty in answering questions, and a feeling of lassitude. Nothing a day or two off duty wouldn't cure.'

'I was thinking of something else.'

'Such as?'

'Radiation sickness.'

Helena Russell was quite positive. 'That was the first thing we checked. I ran a sensor over him straight way. Zoref hasn't been exposed to direct radiation. There's no residual radiation in his body.'

Kano frowned.

'He's fine, David,' insisted Helena Russell.

'I'm glad to hear it. Thanks, Helena.'

He cut off the connection.

'Well, David?' asked Bergman from the screen.

'I'll re-check, Victor. There must be a lead *somewhere.*'

Zoref's return startled his wife. She jumped out of bed and saw him in the living-room.

'I slept through your duty session!' she cried. 'Damn it, I've missed half my shift!' She failed to notice his preoccupation. 'No, it's only half past eight—and you're back—what happened?' She saw that he was swaying. 'Anton?'

'I didn't feel too good. Oh, they checked me over. I'll be fine.'

She watched as he shambled to the heating control. He turned the switch to 'Full'.

'But what happened?'

'Nothing, Eva. But I felt so cold! Just as if I'd been out there'—he indicated the surface above—'without a spacesuit.'

Eva Zoref shivered.

'You think it's cold in here, Anton? I'd say it's stifling. I think I'll dress.' She went to the bedroom.

Zoref got to his feet. The glare of the living-room light held an odd fascination for him. He put out his hands. Within seconds, the lamp dimmed. Then it went blank.

'Sitting in the dark?' asked Eva Zoref, who was more worried than she cared to say. 'Why not go to bed? You'll be warmer, Anton. I'll have a word with Dr Russell. Maybe there's something I can do.'

Her words brought a flare of anger. 'No! No, don't go anywhere—stay here, Eva!'

He lurched to his feet.

'But the doctor said you should rest, didn't she? Come back, Anton!'

Zoref's face in the semi-dark was a twisted mask of pain. 'Stay here, Eva. *Here!*'

Koenig wanted oblivion. They wouldn't leave him alone.

'Look, John,' Bergman was saying. 'Here's the extreme ranging scan—just a blotch. Irregular, a shifting pattern of energies. Almost as if it's in a state of change. Growth, if you like.'

'He's saying it's alive,' said David Kano.

'Yes,' agreed Koenig. They had observed aberrations in space before. Weird energy-sources. The debris of stars blown out ten million years before. So why get worked up over another?

'John, there the other thing too,' said Kano. 'The technician who panicked.'

Morrow felt uncomfortable as he pointed out the facts to the Commander. It wasn't like John to be so slow.

'Look, Commander, you can see there's another coincidental reading,' he said. 'I was going to blast the energy-source just as Technican Zoref pressed the panic button.'

'Three things, John,' said Bergman. 'One, we lose contact with the energy-source. Two, Zoref sees or hears something that scares him so bad he panics. Three, we lose a chunk of energy from his station in Number Two NGA.'

'It should be investigated,' suggested Morrow.

'So investigate,' said Koenig, with an effort.

He tried not to notice the disappointment of the three men.

Dominix was surprised to see Zoref back in the Maintenance Area.

'How are you feeling, Anton? They tell you what's wrong?'

'I'm all right now.' He indicated the shields which held the ferocious radiation in check. 'Did they find anything?'

'An unexplained energy loss. They took all the monitoring tapes, right down to the manual scans. Kano's working on them now.'

'I hope they come up with something.'

'Don't worry about it, Anton! Look, if you're sick, you should be off-duty. Why don't you get the hell out of here and relax?'

'I'm not good at relaxing.'

'You've got a work-fixation, Anton, that's your trouble.'

He walked to the panel and checked the readings. Dominix watched him, then called:

'Want some coffee, Anton?'

Zoref didn't seem to have heard, so Dominix crossed to the recess which housed the coffee-machine. He was more worried about his friend than he admitted to himself. Zoref had the abstraction of the man in shock. When he returned, a steaming cup in each hand, Zoref was shivering violently.

'I'm cold,' he whispered. 'Like death . . .'

Dominix thrust the coffee towards Zoref.

'Drink this. Then back to bed!'

Zoref reached out. He took the cup. Dominix saw what happened but didn't believe it.

The coffee had solidified, frozen, as Zoref took it. Zoref cried out in horror. He dropped the cup. The ball of frozen coffee rolled out, glistening, frosted on the hard floor.

'For God's sake, Anton!' said Dominix. He reached out to touch his friend's shoulder to steady him. A freezing agony shot through his body. He stared at Zoref's contorted face, but the words that formed remained unspoken.

Zoref backed away as Dominix's body shuddered, then stiffened. The face was ghastly white. A white rime of frost covered the whole of the big, solid body. Then Dominix fell with a crash.

Zoref looked down. He saw the medical monitor on his friend's wrist. It was flashing on and off, sending a report to the computer.

The information reached Main Mission Control within seconds. Bergman and Morrow looked towards Commander Koenig. There was a look of unutterable sadness on his lean face.

'Technician N. Dominix,' announced the electronic voice that had soulessly reported so many tragedies. 'Life-functions terminated.

'John,' said Bergman, for he had seen reaction. 'It's Number Two Nuclear Generating Area. First Zoref. Now Dominix. Whatever's hit Alpha is down there.'

CHAPTER NINE

Dr Helena Russell had finished her examination.

'What happened?' asked Bergman.

Two medical attendants wheeled in a trolley. Dominix looked as if he had been lying in a hard frost.

'Death was instantaneous. The cause of death was a sudden decrease in body temperature. If I hadn't known that he was alive four minutes ago, I'd say that he'd been dead for days. I'll have to wait for an autopsy to tell you more. Please move him,' she told the attendants.

'You'll let me have the results as soon as possible?' said Bergman.

'Of course, Victor.'

When she had gone, Bergman looked around the empty generating area. 'It's here, David. Whatever caused that huge drop in temperature is *here*.'

Zoref walked into his living quarters and sat in the swivel chair. He put his head to his hands. Eva Zoref was desperately worried.

'Anton?' she said softly.

He looked up.

'Oh, you're feeling better! I'm glad—'

'Don't come near me!'

She stopped, hurt and puzzled. Anton's behaviour was increasingly strange. He was normally a placid and quietly-spoken man. She bit her lip.

'What's the trouble, darling?'

'Please don't come any nearer,' Zoref said quietly.

She stared at him for a while. Her natural impulse was to comfort him. She put out her hand and might have moved forward but for the sudden announcement from the wall screen. Paul Morrow's urgent tones filled the living-room:

'Calling all personnel! Here is a special announcement, effective immediately. Access to Number Two Nuclear Generating Area is now restricted to those personnel with my direct authorization. Further information will be relayed as soon as possible.'

Eva Zoref looked scared: 'Anton, that's your station. What's happened?'

'Dominix died,' he said flatly.

'Mike Dominix dead! How? And how do you know?'

'I was there.'

'But what happened!'

'Eva, please sit down. Over there.'

Eva Zoref began to protest, but Anton's calmness stopped her.

'There isn't any—You're not in trouble, Anton?'

Zoref shook his head. 'No. It's something I can't explain right now.'

'You are in trouble!' Eva cried, rising.

'*Keep away from me!*'

'You're not well—I'll get Dr Russell, Anton!'

'No, Eva! Sit down! You must trust me! Look Eva, something strange happened in the generating area. I'm not sure what. But you're not to get involved. Now, promise me you'll stay here—'

'Why? Where are you going?' She was ready to defy him.

'I have to—I have to report to Dr Russell. I have some information for her. I'll be back as soon as I can, Eva. Promise me you'll stay?'

His words had a frightening lack of emotion that brought a tingle of fear trickling through Eva Zoref's mind.

'All right,' she heard herself whisper. 'I'll wait. I promise.'

Bergman passed Koenig the plates.

'David Kano found these recorded by an obsolete radiographic-response scanner from the early days of Alpha. It wasn't hooked into the computer's circuits, so we didn't get a report.'

Koenig felt a jolt of interest. The blinding pain relaxed as he glanced at the radiographs.

'The scanner was triggered twice. These plates show what happened,' Bergman told him.

Koenig examined the first.

'It corresponds with the configuration of the energy-source you advised Paul to destroy. Weaker, smaller, but with the same contours,' he said slowly.

'It was taken when Zoref hit the panic-button.'

Koenig held up the second plate.

Bergman explained:

'The time corresponds with the report from computer that Technician Dominix's life-functions had ceased.'

'The same configuration!'

'Yes, John. Whatever hit Zoref and then Dominix is part of the alien energy-source.'

'It's present when Zoref collapsed . . . it's there

again when Dominix dies. And it has the same structure as the energy-source from the gulf.'

'Yes, John. We can't escape the obvious conclusion,' said Bergman. 'An alien force is loose somewhere on Alpha.'

Zoref's physique seemed to have altered. Normally upright, he now lumbered along with a shambling step. His shoulders were rounded, and his arms held at chest-level as though he clasped a great pain. He looked forward from hooded glittering eyes, and his breathing was shallow and rapid. He paused at the doorway leading to the Diagnostic Unit. Dimly, he knew he needed help.

He was distracted by the tap-tapping of a female medical orderly's shoes. She saw him and recognized that he had received treatment.

'How are you—' she said, and then she was aware of the strange brightness about his eyes. Instinctively, she stopped and backed away.

Zoref advanced towards her. She began to walk away from him, too nervous to question him, too proud and confused to rationalize her actions. If she had dared, she would have run. She wasn't frightened enough to scream, and she was too self-assured to admit that her fears might be justified.

Zoref's teeth juddered as the bitter cold sat in his chest like a cancer. He didn't know anything now but the cold.

The medical orderly saw a travel tube station open. Two men looked out. She ran, but the door had closed before they saw her. She screamed then.

About Zoref's head a dim white halation formed. The girl felt the first chill as she battered against the doorway of the travel tube. She turned and saw his face glistening with frost.

He put out his hands.
The lights dimmed.

Helena Russell turned the torch from the frozen face.

'The same as Dominix,' she said to Bergman and Koenig. 'She died instantly from shock as a result of rapid freezing.'

Koenig put a hand to Helena's shoulder.

'She'll be the last. We'll find what's killing them. Get back to medical. I think you'll be needed. David!' he called into his wrist communicator. 'Have you traced the power-fault?'

The lights above sprang into brightness as he spoke. 'Power restored, Commander,' crackled Kano's voice from the speaker overhead.

'Cause?'

'The whole area suffered a sudden drainage of power. It simply leaked away. There's a fault somewhere.'

Bergman looked down at the pitiful corpse. She had been a pleasant girl. He remembered that she had once treated him for a graze on his arm.

'First Dominix and now this girl. What caused Dominix and this girl to die was total heat loss. And now we have the lights losing power.' He burst out suddenly: 'Of course! Lighting uses energy—and heat is energy!'

Koenig understood.

'An energy-consuming alien entity. Is that what we have on Alpha?' he asked.

'It's the only theory that fits the facts!'

'Then let's find it. David!' he called to Kano, with a sudden return to his normal decisiveness. 'Monitor all power levels throughout Alpha. Any fluctuation, I want to know immediately.'

'Got it, Commander,' said Kano.

'Controller Morrow?'

'Hooked in, Commander.'

'Paul, I'm returning to Main Mission Control. Meanwhile station security patrols at every strategic location. Have all off-duty security personnel called out and ready to move on command.'

'Sir!'

'And you, Victor—set the theory up on a probability basis! I want the computer jerked out of its unco-operativeness!'

'I'll do that.' Bergman smiled. 'I think we'll manage now, Commander.'

Eva Zoref hurried through the long corridors. She saw groups of Security guards racing purposefully toward the high-risk areas, power controls, generating and air-conditioning plant, weapons stations. Each man carried sidearms. She reached the Medical Centre minutes after Helena Russell returned.

'Doctor Russell!' she called.

Helena Russell was about to perform an autopsy on the dead medical orderly.

'Not now,' said the senior assistant. 'I'm sorry, the Doctor's too busy—'

'Please! Doctor Russell, let me see him!'

Helena heard and entered the Unit. The senior assistant grabbed Eva Zoref's arm.

'It's Eva Zoref, isn't it?' asked Helena Russell.

Eva broke free of the restraining grip.

'Let me see him, Doctor! He was behaving so oddly!'

'Who—of course, your husband! Technician Zoref, right?'

'Yes! Let me see him, please!'

'But he isn't here—is he?' Helena called.

'No, Doctor,' reported the chief medical assistant.

'No visit by Technician A. Zoref. Not since we examined him earlier.'

'But he said he was coming . . .'

'What's wrong?' said Helena.

'It's Anton. I don't know . . . he's sick! He has been acting so strangely since his accident. And he won't have me near him!' She sobbed. 'I think he's going out of his mind since he saw Mike Dominix killed!'

'Your husband? He was there when it happened? In Number Two Generating Area—can you answer to this, Eva?'

Eva Zoref stared helplessly at the older woman. She knew that she had said too much.

'Commander Koenig!' she heard Dr Russell call urgently. The screen above at the far end of the Centre sprang into life. 'John!'

'I'm busy, Dr Russell. Is it urgent?' Koenig said. 'Will it keep?'

'No! I've got Eva Zoref here! She's just told me that Technician Anton Zoref was present in Number Two Generating Area when Technician Dominix died!'

Koenig put a hand to the scar on his forehead. Helena Russell knew the effort it took him to speak.

'I'll have Professor Bergman interview her—send her to Main Mission.' Koenig stared at Helena Russell for a while. 'And thanks, Helena. It might be the break we need.'

CHAPTER TEN

Bergman's probing questions soon elicited the few facts from Eva Zoref. She was too stunned by the rapidity of events to try to conceal what she knew.

'For Anton's sake, we have to know what happened,' he said. 'We must find him before he comes to further harm. You'd better report to your duty post, Eva. It will give you something to do.'

'I'd rather stay at Main Mission Control.'

'She can stay,' said Koenig. 'Well, Victor?'

'I've just got a read-out from the computer. It confirms what Eva Zoref says. Technician Anton Zoref was in the Maintenance Area of Number Two Generator Nuclear Generator when his colleague Technician Dominix died.'

'Find him, Paul!' snapped Koenig to Morrow. 'Make that the first priority.'

Morrow began to relay instructions.

Zoref was altering. His narrow body was so heavy that he could hardly drag it about. His spine seemed to curve of its own volition. His head was longer, flatter. At times, he would support himself on hands as well as feet. His body was continually wracked by a deep shuddering. Ice crackled from his nose and lips. He moaned in a low, keening voice. But he had cunning.

When the two guards clumped to their station beside

an ancillary air-conditioning plant, he turned into the solarium. The warmth stopped the shuddering, and he walked in upright, almost like a man.

The solarium was skilfully designed to simulate conditions on a calm, semi-tropical beach. Windows usually brought in some light from the stars, but not now that they were in the deep gulfs. The heat and light came from large sun-lamps. Groups of benches and reclining chairs alternated with shaded areas around a swimming-pool. Two women and one man lay on couches, eyes shaded against the brilliant radiation lamps.

The man rolled on to his back, murmured contentedly, and got to his feet. He started to walk in the direction of a shower; Zoref stumbled past him blindly.

'You crazy!' called the man. 'Where's your radiation glasses?'

Zoref was staring directly into the flooding light. His shuddering became a violent spasm of relief. The man, an electronics expert, felt the chill spreading from Zoref. He shivered.

Zoref reached upwards.

Overhead, the powerful lamps wavered, dimmed, and died. The chill hit the two sleeping women. They awoke to semi-darkness and saw the grey-black figure of Zoref, poised like a diver with his arms high above them. He was producing grating sounds that had no relationship to human speech.

The electronics expert forced himself to take a step nearer. Behind him, the two women hugged their robes about them. One panicked and screamed. The man backed away from the wall of freezing air.

'Solarium!' he yelled into his wrist communicator. 'We've got power trouble—Johnson of electronics speaking! Get a power maintenance crew up here!'

'Commander,' said a female technician to Koenig. 'Urgent. Power fluctuations reported.'

Kano rapidly scanned the readings.

'It's the solarium, John!'

Paul Morrow was already deploying a force of Security men. 'I'll go!' he called to Koenig.

'You stay here!' ordered Koenig. 'I'm going up!'

'Take this!' yelled Morrow.

Koenig turned. The stubby weapon was altogether out of keeping with the situation. Nevertheless, he took the laser-beam projector.

'Thanks, Paul. I hope it won't be necessary.'

Zoref turned blind eyes towards the screaming women. The women's bodies radiated fear. And heat.

He advanced towards them, arms outstretched.

Then the Security guards burst in, hand-guns drawn.

'Hold it, Zoref!' a sergeant yelled. 'Zoref, don't move!'

Johnson grabbed the two women, who had seemed unable to move. He pushed them roughly towards the entrance.

Zoref waited.

'Don't shoot him!' yelled Koenig, bursting through the group of Security men as the radiation lamps glowed dimly into life.

Zoref stared towards the light-source, puzzlement showing in his thin face. He reached up again. A guard couldn't control his shaking hands, and a laser jet scoured the wall behind Zoref. Koenig kicked out and the hand-gun shot into the air. It clattered to the ground, spinning.

'Blast the radiation lamps!' Koenig yelled.

He aimed the stubby weapon at the dim lights. A jet lanced out, blasting the heat-lamp into fragments.

The guards understood. In seconds, the solarium was dark again.

Zoref groaned, then collapsed.

The two women pushed through the guards. Koenig patted Johnson on the arm but he did not speak to him. There was time for congratulations later.

'Dr Russell to the solarium,' he ordered. 'We've found Zoref.'

The great hall was cold. Koenig looked out at the reaches of sable blackness beyond the windows. *Alien,* he thought, and Zoref's coldness hit him too. *Alien, hungry for energy. An entity from that deep emptiness. Was that what had possession of Zoref?*

Helena Russell arrived within two minutes.

She carried a portable life-functions decoder. Its antennae quivered as she examined Zoref.

'He's alive,' she said after a puzzled silence. 'I don't know what damage he's suffered—look at his skull! And the radiation burns!'

'He's absorbed a huge amount of energy,' said Koenig. He shone a torch over Zoref's thin features.

'Careful!' warned Helena Russell. 'Don't touch him—it could be lethal.'

Koenig looked at the beam of his torch. It was stable.

'He's not absorbing energy now. I want him moved for examination, Helena. I think he's safe for the moment, but use robot grabs to move him to Diagnostic. I'm taking no chance with the orderlies. Two dead is enough. More than enough. And use a restraint harness on him—something he can't get out of.'

'I'll be careful, John,' said Helena Russell.

She was thinking that Koenig sounded like the old Commander of Moonbase Alpha once more. His eyes were steady and clear, his orders decisive. She pushed these thoughts from her mind and arranged

for Zoref's transfer with her normal controlled profes-
sionalism.

An hour later, she had completed her examination.
She called Main Mission Control.

'I have the plates ready,' she said. 'Technician
Zoref is under observation. I've taken the precaution
of having him strapped down, but I'm not sure it's
necessary.'

'Let me see him,' said Koenig.

The man appeared to be asleep. His face had not
been bandaged, but a layer of some plastic dressing
gave him a waxen appearance. A single blue light
picked out the gaunt features. Steel bands held him
at the shoulders, waist and thighs.

'He's losing heat all the time,' said Helena Russell.
'I've tried to maintain a constant body temperature,
but his metabolism keeps altering. There's something
uncanny about it. As if he doesn't want to stabilize
at normal heat.'

Koenig waited until Bergman had examined the
plates:

'What do you make of it, Victor?'

Bergman passed the plates to Koenig.

'There,' he said. 'See—these dark patches are Zoref's
bones and thicker tissue. See how the skull is massively
reinforced. And now look inside the cranial cavity.'

Koenig peered closer. He saw a small grey-black
blotch, hardly larger than a toe-nail.

'Is that it?'

'It has the configuration of the ailen energy-source.'
Bergman could not keep the excitement from his voice.
'It's the force that killed Dominix and the girl. I haven't
compared it with the original scans for computer analysis—I'll relay the plates now—but I'm sure of it.'

'But why does it lodge there? Why in Zoref?'

'Who knows? Maybe Zoref was a convenient host

or the right kind of catalyst. At any rate, it seems to be dormant now, John. We'll have a chance of studying—'

'No! I want it rooted out of Zoref's body! While we've got a chance of controlling it, we'll destroy it—immediately.'

'But John, we can't do that! Not to an unexplained life-form—'

'Have you forgotten your original advice? You were the one who wanted it blasted, Victor.'

'I was, but then it threatened Alpha, or it seemed to.' Bergman indicated the slack form. 'Does *that* seem to be a threat to Moonbase Alpha?'

Koenig touched the scar on his forehead. The pain was near again. He refused to acknowledge its nearness:

'Get Kano to set up a computer analysis of possible methods for destruction. I don't want Zoref harmed, naturally. But I want that *thing* rooted out!'

Bergman stared back angrily for a moment. Then:

'Yes, Command—'

He stopped, aghast. Zoref's head seemed to glow with an eerie grey-black radiance.

'Guards!' Morrow was already calling.

Koenig shouted: 'Lasers, full power!' as Zoref's arms stiffened against the steel bands. He opened his arms, and the bright steel flew back, shattered. He raised his legs, and the steel confining them shivered. At his waist, the powerful bands of metal held for a second or two, then they gave in a ringing spray of razor-edged fragments.

Zoref stood up and looked at the blue light. He reached a hand to touch it.

The screen went black.

'Emergency in Medical Centre!' reported an electronic voice.

Kano heard. He had a read-out in his hand:

'John, computer wants us to—'

'Not now!' he snapped. 'Paul, get a report from the Medical deck!'

'Coming in now, Commander,' said Morrow tightly.

'Guard Sullivan!' a hoarse voice called. 'The man's gone stark crazy! He's reaching to the lights and they're all failing—Now he's over at the power-controls—he's hurt, he's reeling! There's a sort of smoke-screen around him. I'll grab him, Controller—'

'Don't try it!' roared Koenig. Echoing him, Morrow yelled: 'Laser, Sullivan—gun him down!'

There was no answer from the guard.

Seconds passed. An unimpassioned voice rang hollowly through Main Mission Control.

'*Security Guard P. Sullivan. Life-functions now terminated. Detailed report follows—*'

'Later!' called Koenig. 'Turn the damned thing off!'

Kano punched commands, and the macabre catalogue of fatal symptoms ceased. It was enough that Sullivan had died. They all knew how they would find him.

'Get down there,' Koenig said to Bergman. 'See if there's any indication of where Zoref's heading for. I'll alert Alpha. And take no chances, Victor!'

Bergman nodded. Koenig wasn't in the mood for argument, not now. The body-count was up to three.

'Attention all personnel,' Koenig called. 'All Moonbase Alpha personnel, this is Commander John Koenig. Now listen!'

News of Zoref's sickness had spread throughout the huge complex. The details weren't known, but the size of the pursuit operation clearly indicated the seriousness of Zoref's condition. Men and women stopped what they were doing. They listened to their Commander in tense and fearful anticipation.

'Technician Zoref is under medical supervision. He has received a massive overdose of radiation, and he is in a dangerous condition. That danger extends to all Alphans. Technician Zoref is a danger to each and every one of you! He is not, repeat *not*, to be approached, except by Security sections. Side-arms have been issued and a shoot-to-kill authorization exists in case of attack. Technician Zoref has been responsible for the deaths of three Alphans, so I give you this warning again: keep away from *Zoref!* If you sight Zoref,' concluded Koenig, 'report the news at once! Stay at your posts and report sightings to Main Mission Control!'

'Orders, Commander?' asked Morrow.

'Make sure your Security details know what to do.'

Bergman returned.

'Sullivan was frozen to death,' he said. 'What now, John?'

Professor Bergman looked his years. His face was grey.

'You and David Kano keep a check on all power losses. Zoref's in need of energy. I want all reports channelled through to you. Plot them on a Moonbase map. I want to know where he's heading for!'

The first losses were already coming through.

'This is Alpha Section B,' said a calm voice. 'We have major losses in all store-rooms. Power loss critical.'

A technician reported the blacking-out of a main corridor. A scanner reported the failure of a communication network through power-loss.

Two female orderlies wanted to know why their laundry unit wouldn't operate, and why they'd been left in the dark.

Koenig stared at the plot which Bergman and Kano

were building up from the information they had received.

'It's not enough!' Koenig burst out. 'The alien was dormant for a while then it adapted to Zoref's metabolism! We've got to stop it growing!'

'Agreed,' said Bergman, looking up, 'It can absorb all the power Alpha produces. See. Already Section A is out. Zoref's moving through B Section and all power-sources fail with his progress.'

'I want him isolated from all energy sources,' said Koenig. 'David,' he said quickly to Kano. 'How quickly can we shut down all Moonbase power?'

Kano was startled.

'You mean *all* Moonbase power?'

'Just that. Cut the alien from power sources and it seems to incapacitate it. I want all power stopped long enough to make the alien vulnerable again.'

'You mean shut down the reactors?'

'No. Just cut the power supply from them.'

'It would take a few seconds, Commander . . .'

'Survival factor?'

Kano knew his technological resources and their limits. 'Without power, in twenty minutes the sick in Intensive Care Units will die. In theory, the recycling plants will be beyond repair. At forty, our oxygen starts to run out . . . any more, Commander?'

Koenig shook his head. The choice was between certain death within forty-five minutes and the danger from Zoref. Deep within him was the conviction that Zoref constituted the more pressing threat.

'Has Zoref been located yet?'

Paul-Morrow looked at the Moonbase map.

'Last traced there,' he said, pointing to the big quadrant that encompassed Sections D and E.

Koenig watched Morrow's hand trail over the chart.

'It's *there*!' he exclaimed, striking his head in anger.

'Why didn't we see it? There—the generating area!
He knows Number Two Generating Area! That's
his duty station! And once he gets there we can't
stop him from blowing the reactors one by one! He's
got to be slowed down!'

'Well?' said Kano.

'Cut all power.'

Eva Zoref had worked it out too.

She knew her husband's dedication to his work.
Anton would be making for his post. She was too
afraid to ask herself why.

CHAPTER ELEVEN

Helena Russell implored Koenig to restore power.
He refused. A patient died soon afterwards. Koenig
heard the news with a stone face as he clambered
over trolleys left about for want of power. There
was no light at all. It might have been a totally deserted
base.

Koenig shone his powerful torch as he heard a
noise ahead.

Three technicians who had been asleep when
Koenig began issuing his emergency orders had tumbled blearily into a corridor to report to their maintenance units when a massive, swollen figure lumbered
down Corridor Twenty-five towards them. *Zoref. And
yet not Zoref.*

There was a great grey-black halation where a

head should be. The thing walked slowly on heavy metallic beam-like legs. There was nothing to connect it with Technician Zoref but a frenzied pair of eyes.

Sensibly, the technicians turned and ran.

Koenig and Bergman appeared as the three men raced past. 'Wait!' snapped Koenig, but it took a flying leap by a Security guard to stop the last man. The others scattered.

'What have you seen—Zoref?'

The man was almost beyond words:

'Zoref?' he gasped. 'Was *that* Zoref—Christ, Commander, it's monstrous!'

'How was he moving—slow, fast?'

'Slow—it was like a dying animal!'

'Heading where?'

'The generating area—Number Two!'

Koenig let him go.

'Commander,' yelled an excited Security man. 'A woman!'

She had appeared from a side corridor, running fast. Koenig sprang forward.

Zoref heard sounds behind him. Ahead was the massive door of the generating area. He limped slowly forward. He placed a limb to the door. It shook free beneath the pressure he exerted. He didn't know he had smashed it down.

The scanners were alive. He saw the glow of the core, where sat unlimited heat, ecstatic living energy. He set up a horrible, sobbing noise as Eva Zoref ran through the debris of the door.

'Anton!' she called, screaming above the noise.

He turned. The great grey-black mass of his head pivoted. In a tiny and residual part of his psyche he knew her.

The sounds from the orifice that had been his mouth came to her. Two syllables. 'Eva.'

'What's happened?' she screamed, appalled. 'Anton? Anton!'

She had seen the head now, the metallic-coated body, the tree-like limbs gleaming dully in the half-light of fission. And still she went to him.

Koenig grabbed her as she moved forward.

'Don't let them kill him!' she screamed.

Koenig thrust her towards one of the Security men. He heard the terrible agony of the thing that had been Zoref. It crawled now, closer, closer, to the controls of the nuclear generator, a pitiable thing.

'Get back, Zoref!' roared Koenig.

Zoref inched forward, huge and elephantine.

Koenig raised the hand-gun.

'Don't fire, John!' yelled Bergman.

Koenig ignored him. He took aim.

'You'll regenerate it!' Bergman was yelling, in the grip of one of the guards. 'John!'

A golden-yellow stream spat from the weapon. It splayed over the dim grey-black blotch. Incredibly, the huge skull turned, so that Zoref stared straight into the jetting beam of power.

And Zoref opened his mouth.

'John!' yelled Bergman.

Koenig understood then. Even as he released his grip on the trigger, he knew that he had been terribly wrong. For the alien that had absorbed Zoref was more powerful now. It had grown. Grotesque energies whirled about the head. The massive body was firmer, the legs stronger.

Zoref reached a grab-like appendage towards a red-painted lever.

'He's opening the reactor!' Bergman shouted. 'Clear the area—get out, John! There's nothing we can do now!'

Koenig heard the roar of the furnace as the dampers shifted in the central core.

'It's going critical, John,' Bergman said quietly. 'We have to evacuate the entire area. With luck, we can isolate the effects.'

Koenig heard Eva Zoref screaming.

'Out!' he called to the Security guards. 'Immediate to Controller Morrow—restore all power from generators One and Three. Emergency screens around Nuclear Generating Area Two. Prepare for nuclear fission!'

No one needed to be told twice. Bergman, the guards with Eva Zoref firmly in their grip, and the technicians sent down by Kano were all running from the danger area. Lights suddenly sprang out at them. They could move faster.

The first dull thuds came to them from far down the corridor as the emergency screens thudded into place around Zoref's generator . . .

The explosion, when it came, had been controlled.

The safety devices worked. Number One Generator rumbled dangerously, but the housing held. A foolish young technician forgot to put on his radiation suit and died as a result. But the power levels held, and there was no sign that the alien entity would raid the two remaining generators.

After three minutes, damage reports tailed off and the Alphans could look at one another with wonder at their survival and curiosity about the alien from the gulf. Most of the Alphans saw it leave.

One of the satellite scanners picked it up first, and then surface scanners homed in.

It wasn't at all remarkable: a grey-black blotch against the sable of the gulf. Not quite the same structure as it had been originally, but recognizable from the first sightings.

By this time, everyone knew that Zoref and the alien were one.

'We're going to be all right,' Bergman said, when

the alien was at the limit of the scanners' range. Its speed was increasing rapidly. 'I wonder where poor Zoref's gone?'

'And what he is,' said Helena Russell.

'If it had got to the other reactors . . .' Kano shuddered.

'One was enough for it,' said Koenig. He touched the scar on his head. When he had the time, he would get it removed. 'The one reactor contained enough energy for its purposes. Wouldn't you say so, Victor?'

'I don't know. Maybe Zoref had something to do with it—maybe he had a curious relationship with that one reactor which didn't extend to the others. I just don't know. But I do know that we're seeing something truly remarkable, John. Maybe a cosmic event that will affect us in the future.'

'Like the birth of a star?' asked Morrow.

Bergman frowned:

'I wonder. Maybe something like that . . . yes . . .'

'Maybe something more,' said Koenig quietly. He was thinking of the purple city now, but calmly. And when he remembered the life that could have been his with the gold honey-bronze woman he sighed. But there was no blinding pain. Dreams would have to suffice.

In the Medical Centre Eva Zoref refused sedation.

Helena Russell called to see her an hour after the disappearance of the grey-black blotch.

'Everybody tried their best, Eva,' she said. 'We just didn't know how to help. If it's any consolation to you, Professor Bergman thinks that Anton wasn't totally absorbed. There's still something left of him out there.'

Eva Zoref crossed to the window.

'Out there,' she said.

'Eva, we're crossing deep space. There are so many things we can't understand. We don't know what this alien force is, nor why it selected Anton, but we're left, you and I and the rest of the Alphans . . .'

'But not Anton.'

'No,' said Helena. 'You have to accept it. And try to help the rest of us accept it. Just as we will try to help you.'

She left the young woman quietly. Maybe time would help. She hoped so.

CHAPTER TWELVE

The gulf seemed to have swallowed them.

At first, the Alphans hardly noticed the great darkness into which the Moon was plunging. There was too much to do. Number One Generator had to be rebuilt. Until they could count on its mighty reserves of power, the Alphans knew their lives were threatened.

Two generators were adequate for the normal Moonbase services, and even then, in an emergency, their output could be lifted. But any one of a dozen malfunctions might put one of the generators off-stream and should that happen when some unknown contingency necessitated a sudden surge of power, there was nothing in reserve.

They needed Zoref's generator. And it had to be

rebuilt from the smallest retaining bolts to the colossal lead screens.

Koenig did not harry the Alphans. David Kano had every one of his technicians working double shifts. There were more than enough volunteers to man the service machines around the clock.

It took a hundred and six hours, and then the eerie fires glowed sullenly again in the confines of the screens.

'Commander, can you get down here,' a tired Kano asked during one long watch.

'Gladly,' said Koenig and meant it.

There was no ceremony, though every one of the technicians who had worked on the generator was there.

'Your privilege, Commander,' said David Kano, indicating the switch which would release the flow of power into the great complex of systems.

'What took so long?' he called. 'A little job like this—now if it had been something serious . . .'

The rest of his words were lost in the laughter.

When they were quiet again Koenig said:

'I never doubted you could do it. Thanks, my thanks to you all.'

Quietly, the technicians watched him press the switch. They drifted away when the generator began to pump its vital and massive energies into the heart of Moonbase Alpha.

David Kano stayed. He looked at Koenig closely.

'You've had the scar fixed,' he said.

Koenig nodded.

It was time he came to terms with the loss of Vana and the brilliant civilization of the Zennites.

'One generator repaired, one scar healed. It took about the same length of time.'

Kano's eyes were half closed.

'Now get some sleep,' Koenig ordered. 'You and the rest of the Technical Sections. You deserve it.'

He remembered something when he was on his way back to Main Mission Control. He stopped off at Medical Centre.

'Well, you're looking fine!' called Helena Russell. 'You know, in a few days the skin-graft will be completely absorbed. Not a sign of rejection.'

'I didn't come about that. How's Technician Eva Zoref?'

Helena crossed to him. 'How long did it take you to get over what happened on Zenno?'

Koenig looked into the calm blue eyes. He was surprised to see a strong reaction there. She was seeing him as a man again, not a patient. He was about to tell Helena Russell that his experiences on Zenno were in no way similar to Eva Zoref's loss of a man who had become possessed by an aberrant creature from the void, but he stopped.

There was a parallel—loss.

'So she'll never recover?' he said.

'Never is too long. She's busy working and she's apparently adjusted to the idea of her husband's transmutation. But until she can say to herself that there's a life for her, there will only be grief and guilt and longing.'

'I'll see she's kept busy,' Koenig said.

'It worked in your case.'

They looked at one another for a while, and then Koenig was conscious of the interested gaze of a young female orderly. Obviously, she had never seen the Medical Director in quite such a light before.

'Dr Russell, I'll look in again.'

Helena Russell saw the change in his expression.

'Any time, Commander.'

She watched him go, a tall, straight-backed man with an easy walk and a certain quiet confidence that soothed her and yet made her pulse quicken whenever she saw him. Given other circumstances, she thought. Given the time and the place, and the absence of pressures . . .

She too noticed the young orderly.

'Now you,' Helena told her, 'can get down to Diagnostic *fast!*'

The girl hastened about her duties. She was still smiling, though. *Dr Russell and the Commander back together? Now, how would that sound to the rest of the girls?*

Koenig told the Section chief to ply Eva Zoref with sheer hard work. It was all he could do for her now.

During the day cycles that followed, the Alphans caught up on their lost sleep. A week drifted by, and soon the routine maintenance of Moonbase was in hand again. A system of random checks had been instituted to guard against an over-reliance on instrumentation; the checks turned up very little, but the exercise was a useful one. It kept the Technical crews busy and it created an additional confidence amongst the rest of the Alphans.

Gradually, however, the sense of isolation began to oppress them. The deep sable of the gulf had a bleakly depressing effect on men and women who were used to the diamond tracery of stars.

There were no clouds of star-debris; no stray asteroids on their lonely journeys around the massive star-systems; no flaring of supernovae into awesome majesty: there was nothing to see but the funereal reaches of dead-black space.

Koenig noticed the edginess amongst the lower grades of Service personnel. The girl who brought the coffee had lost her cheerfulness. The woman who collected the laundry looked positively sullen. And Dr Russell reported three cases of drug-stealing. It was the sleep-inducing pills that went. She suspected one of the orderlies and had her transferred to other duties.

The thefts stopped, but the morning clinic became a lengthy affair. Staff complained of dizziness, headaches, sleeplessness.

'Classic disorientation symptoms,' Bergman told Koenig, when they looked at the sick-returns. 'They can be induced in any black box experiment. What we're getting now is a response to a feeling of total isolation.' He pointed to the forward con. 'When *I* look out there, I feel we're heading for the end of Creation. If I let myself dream about it, I'd ask for happy-pills too.'

Helena Russell agreed.

'We're used to trouble. The Alphans are conditioned to violent action, to emergencies—they, we, can cope with trouble.' She too looked at the oppressive dark. 'If I thought there was a God, I'd say He's lost us.'

Koenig touched the side of his head. The skin was unblemished, yet there was still a tingling of remembrance. Both Bergman and Helena were right. No one had time for traumas when Moonbase was under siege. Isolation and inaction were the subtler enemies. Koenig called the Section chiefs to discuss ways of counter-acting the loss of morale.

'Tighten maintenance procedures,' Koenig ordered. 'Get a new programme of checks for the Eagles. And run pilot courses for anyone interested,' he told Paul Morrow. 'I want everyone *busy*.'

'I could offer medical training for a limited number,' said Helena Russell.

'Advanced computer analysis,' Kano said.

Koenig nodded.

'Anyone else?'

'Simulated astro-readings,' Bergman offered. 'Useful if we ever see the stars again.'

Koenig smiled. There was no edge of bitterness in Bergman's voice. He hadn't cracked.

'Flower arrangement?' someone muttered.

Koenig looked up sharply. A fattish service engineer of considerable seniority was looking intently at the floor.

'If it keeps someone off drugs, then yes, flower arrangement!' Koenig called.

'First find your flowers,' someone else muttered, and this time there was a hint of despair. Koenig ignored it.

'We're beyond the islands in deep space,' he said. 'We're out beyond the range of Earth's furthest-ranging scanners, but that shouldn't worry us. Keep it firmly before your Sections—there's no way back for us! We go where the Moon's flight-path takes us, and we live with it. Make sure that every last man and woman on Moonbase Alpha understands: until we're across the gulf, there can be no more talk of a future anywhere except here, on this planet, on this base, right here! There's nothing, but nothing, out there!'

Only ten hours later, Koenig wondered at the irony of it all.

Normally a heavy sleeper, he was in only a light and semi-conscious state when the news broke:

'Commander to Main Mission Control!' a voice was calling urgently. 'Commander Koenig to Main Mission Control!'

Koenig rolled over and sprang to his feet.

'Report!' he called to the excited duty officer.

David Kano's smiling features appeared:

'You've got to come up here to see it, John! It's showing better all the time!'

Koenig fastened his belt. Jumbled ideas slipped

through his mind. What had turned David Kano into a grinning idiot? Why the insane reports? Was everyone at Main Mission on some sort of hypno-jag? Had they been feeding one another happy-pills?

He looked at the screen again. Bergman was gesticulating with all the elegance of an animated scarecrow:

'John, we're getting long-range scans, and the data shows it's a planet-sized mass!'

Koenig's heart jerked. Hope flooded through him. So, after all, the gulf was not empty!

He raced to Main Mission Control, to find it filling with jubilant Alphans.

'Let's have it!' he called, pushing past a gaggle of Service engineers who had no right at all to invade the nerve-centre of the Moonbase complex.

'It's genuine, Commander,' called Paul Morrow, his large red face split by a huge grin. 'I don't know how or why an isolated planet and a small star should have got out there, but they are—just coming into visual range now!'

Koenig could have sung. Not much smaller than Earth. A hot-enough sun. And simulated visual patterns showing a gaseous envelope.

'It's the jackpot!' Kano shouted. 'We've hit it—we've got lucky, right out here in the gulf!'

Koenig held back for a while, but the emotions of the Alphans caught him up.

'We'll have a closer look at it,' he said. 'I'll clear an exploratory mission. Paul, detail two men and a survey Eagle.'

'Right away, Commander!'

'And clear Main Mission! This is a working-space, not a viewing gallery!'

A security section-leader recollected his duties and began easing the excited Alphans out of Main Mission Control. Technicians calmed and settled to their consoles. Within a couple of minutes, the big desk was a scene of quiet concentration. Yet, in the low-humming quietness, a whisper came to Koenig's ear:

'How about that flower-arrangement!'

Again, Koenig employed a commander's privilege to adjust his hearing-levels. And he could marvel at the turn-around of events. Isolation had been about to induce a general despair; this new sighting had come at exactly the right moment.

He checked with Bergman and Kano before making the confirmatory announcement of what everyone already knew. It was unnecessary, but there had to be a due form to acknowledge the change in events.

'This is Commander John Koenig,' he announced. 'Our scanners have ranged on a planet a little above Earth's dimensions, and with an attendant sun that is enough to give it the possibility of an Earth-type atmosphere and climatic conditions.' He waited and his tone changed. 'I don't think that's news to any Alphan. I can tell you now that computer has advised the sending of an exploratory mission, and I have ordered a survey Eagle to stand by. But I ask that there be no undue optimism! We've been fooled before. If this is the real thing, then we all have a cause for rejoicing. For the moment, let's wait.' Koenig allowed himself a smile. 'All Alphans not engaged on essential duties have permission to view events as they occur.'

CHAPTER THIRTEEN

'Now that, John, was a good move,' Professor Bergman said, immediately after Koenig's announcement. 'It's going to make everybody feel involved. The raw edges were beginning to show.'

Koenig's hand went instinctively to the site of the scar. It was quite smooth. He felt himself whole again. His own raw edges had healed.

'Well, David,' he asked Kano, 'what are the chances?'

Kano frowned.

'Nothing beyond the initial recommendation to send out a survey Eagle. Computer won't say that the planet is viable for humans. See.' He indicated the latest read-outs. 'Everything from a projected breathable atmosphere with temperate climates to a planet of ashes and dust.'

'That's computers,' Bergman put in. 'They take account of probabilities, come up with extreme variations of interpretations, and then sit on the fence when you ask for a definite answer.'

'They just don't care!' Paul Morrow said. 'The only way is to send out the survey party.'

'Your recommendations for pilots?' asked Koenig.

'Myself as first pilot and—'

'Not you, Paul,' said Koenig quietly.

Morrow's face expressed dismay. He didn't argue, though.

'Barker as first, Irving as co-pilot, Commander.'

'Barker's steady enough, but Irving?'

'Noisy, but good in an emergency. He's got the quickest reactions in the whole of Reconnaissance. And Barker will keep him quiet.'

Irving was an extrovert, something of a joker. It was an important mission, perhaps the most important Eagle survey ever. Koenig hesitated for a moment.

'Have them sent up here, Paul.'

The men were eager to carry out their mission. Irving's dark eyes gleamed with excitement. Barker's large, solid shape was taut with tension.

'You understand, I want no heroics,' Koenig said. 'Your instructions will come through computer. Get the atmosphere and surface samples just as computer directs. No private forays, no souvenir-hunting. You'll stick to the flight-path the computer gives you. Controller Carter tells me you're the best team for the job. Prove it.'

'We will, sir,' said Barker.

'Commander, count the goods as already delivered!' Irving grinned.

'Good luck,' Koenig said, shaking both men by the hand. Irving's grin was infectious. Everyone on the desk was caught up in the little man's enthusiasm.

'Launch Pad Six,' a technician called. 'Eagle Six ready for launch, Commander.'

The two men hurried away, the shorter man leading.

'I wanted to see them,' Koenig told Paul Morrow. 'Now I have, I'm satisfied. They'll do.'

There was silence in Main Mission Control as the graceful shape of the survey Eagle filled the big screen. Two space-suited figures clambered up the ramp. The difference in size between them was emphasized by the bulky orange Reconnaissance suits. Koenig could see that Irving was still grinning.

'Ready for launching, Commander,' reported the flight director.

'Launch,' ordered Koenig.

The Eagle rode on twin gouts of white fire for a few-seconds, then it climbed like a huge dragonfly into the blackness.

Orbital scanners recorded its flight beyond the Moon's horizon. There were only a few whispered comments, until the scanners showed the tiny skeletal shape lifting clear of the Moon and making for the dark planet.

'Eagle Six on flight-path,' reported an electronic voice. 'No malfunctions.'

'A perfect launch,' said David Kano. 'The new maintenance schedules paid off.'

Koenig relaxed. 'Pass the word to the Service technicians. Congratulations on their efficiency. It's the first time I've heard a "no malfunctions" from computer.'

It was unusual. Normally, some tiny system would show a fault, and it was not uncommon for computer to complain about major deficiencies. By the nature of their construction, the Eagles were prone to malfunctions. Light in weight, their two massive engines imposed tremendous strains on the fabric of the ships. Constant servicing reduced the potential hazards, but still bugs showed up.

Koenig felt a glow of pleasure. The venture had begun well.

'How about predictions on the planet now?' he asked Kano.

'It's refusing to give definite forecasts,' Kano told him. He looked puzzled. 'We're nearer now, and computer's getting direct information through the Eagle Six Link. It won't even make a best guess.'

'See if they're getting anything with the onboard computer,' Koenig ordered.

'Yes, Commander,' said the technician at the big screen console. 'Mission Control to Eagle Six. Pilot Barker, report onboard readings to Commander.'

The big screen shivered with spangling sunlight and then Irving's dark face gazed back at the Main Mission crewmen:

'It's looking just great!' he shouted. 'Readings—we don't need them! We have visuals!'

Barker turned from the controls.

'Commander, we've got it made here! I'm going into low orbit for final descent, then we'll relay direct sightings.'

'Final descent?' Koenig echoed. 'They can't be near the planet yet!'

'I heard that, Commander—we made good time, eh?' called Irving. 'Eagle Six is one fine ship, you can tell the Service crews from Bud Irving!'

Kano was already checking the ship's location. Bergman started to say something, but Irving's loud yell blotted out the words:

'Take her through *that*!'

'I see it,' Barker said, the tension back in his voice. 'Commander, I see a break in the cloud cover. We're going through now.'

Koenig heard the cheering from beyond Main Mission Control as the Alphans caught a glimpse of the planet's surface, a rolling, green and wooded land blurred in mist and rain.

'Turn that noise down!' he snapped to the screen technician. 'David—they can't be at the planet yet! They're two hours ahead of schedule according to the computer's flight-path.'

Kano passed him the read-out which had just emerged from the console in front of him.

'Computer doesn't query the flight. According to computer, Eagle Six is dead on schedule.'

'No Eagle could have gone that fast,' Carter said. The jubilation was gone from the faces of the men and women in Main Mission, as they realized what Koenig was saying. 'The Eagle would have blown,' Carter went on. 'It just isn't possible!'

'Yet computer says—' began Kano.

'Computer's wrong!' Koenig snapped.

Bergman said slowly:

'Computers like this one *can't* be wrong. Unless . . .'

'Unless they're fed wrong information!' Kano cried. 'I'll check with calculators!'

It would take hours, Koenig realized.

Nothing could take the place of the fantastic capabilities of the main computer at Moonbase Alpha.

Into the quietness came Irving's voice, high-pitched but with a lesser volume:

'Je-*sus*! Do you see that?'

In a bowl of shallow hills was a jumble of ruined buildings. And, rearing from amongst them a great black tower.

'We have artefacts,' said Barker. 'Commander, I see a regular shape, maybe a hundred metres high, apparently artificial. The regular shapes you see around it look as though they might have been buildings. We're going to hold orbit for a look-see.'

'This is a weirdie from way back!' yelled Irving. 'And are we moving!'

'Going into descent orbit—' Barker said.

Koenig acted without consciously making a decision. Instinctively he knew that the venture, which had begun with such apparent success, was doomed. Times were wrong. Speeds. The planet's surface.

Green, and then, clawing at the edges of vision, black ash, broken rock, rolling dust . . .

Wrong!

'Eagle Six!' Koenig roared. 'Abort mission—do not go into descent orbit! This is Koenig—Barker, pull out of descent dive!"

'John, what's happening out there?' called Bergman.

Koenig ignored him.

'I say again, Barker, abort your mission—*pull out*!'

Bergman caught his arm.

'It doesn't look too bad. We're getting good readings now from computer. See, computer's come up with a decision. It's a habitable planet—'

Koenig impatiently shook his arm free.

'Paul, do we have to hook-up with the Eagle? Are they receiving Main Mission?'

Morrow checked quickly.

'There's a clear, direct reciprocal link.'

'Then why doesn't Barker answer?'

'Abort mission, Eagle Six!' roared Koenig once more.

The screen still showed Irving, but he had turned away. He was staring raptly at the planetary surface as if seeing visions.

'Look at those readings!' Koenig said helplessly.

He pointed to the console which monitored the onboard readings from Eagle Six.

Morrow paled.

'It can't pull out at that speed!' Morrow said. 'Barker, this is Controller Morrow!' he roared to the unheeding pilots aboard Eagle Six. 'Your orders are to pull out. Mission aborted—get out of that dive!'

'They're in too close, sir!' yelled a technician.

'They're going to smear themselves all over the surface! The G-forces are too much! They're out of control!'

Kano was wrestling with the calculators, his fingers racing over the manual keyboard at an unbelievable rate.

'John, there's a discrepancy—the computer isn't recording what's happening down there!'

Koenig sighed. It was the greatest irony of all. The machine which revered perfection was itself malfunctioning.

"How, John *how*!" demanded Morrow.

'G-forces increasing rapidly,' said the now white-faced technician. 'They can't live through it.'

'And still computer says everything's fine down there!' called Kano, as he tore off a new read-out. 'There's a continuing and increasing discrepancy in every reading, John!'

Koenig made one last attempt.

Quietly, he said:

'If you read this, Eagle Six pilots, pull out now. If you can make it, use emergency capsule ejection. You are in crash-dive configuration. The G-forces are seven above computer's estimate. Get out!'

Irving turned. He hadn't lost his impudent grin.

'Now, Commander, what is all the sweat about? Anyone would think we have trouble. And have we, Ed?'

'Trouble is one thing we've none of,' said Barker confidently. He turned to smile at the watchers in Main Mission. 'Little Bud here's right. Now, we may be flying a little low for comfort, but it's one great trip.'

'Barker!' said Morrow. 'That can't be Barker!'

'Controller, just enjoy the ride with us!' Irving called. 'Just imagine it's free-flight back on Earth!'

'Be our guests,' invited Barker. 'And my diminutive co-pilot has it right again. Why, we're regularly swanning down to that cool green planet, my fellow Alphans, and soon we'll bring you a few chunks of it back!'

The long range scanners picked up the Eagle's flight-track. Curved lines represented the sickeningly fast crash-dive.

'They've gone mad,' said Kano. 'Space-happy—abort,' he muttered. 'Abort!' And all of the Main Mission crew joined in the plea to the smiling pilots of Eagle Six.

'Sailing clear and easy,' said Barker. 'Commander, there must be some kind of computer foul-up. We've no problems about rapid descent. In fact, I've rarely known an easier approach, sir.'

'I just looked out at a little lake,' Irving called gleefully. 'When we get out, I'm throwing this suit away and going for a swim!'

Barker called out, just as eagerly:

'Commander, did you see the tower? Did you *see* it?'

His voice was full of awe.

'It's the ejector now,' Koenig said, his voice rock-steady. 'You can just make it.'

'But the tower—did you see it?'

Koenig humoured him.

'We missed that, Ed. Now get yourself and Bud Irving out—*fast*!'

As he said it, the screen emptied.

A last whooping laugh came from the doomed ship. Hearing it, the watchers grew cold.

'How does it read?' Koenig asked Paul Morrow.

'You don't need a read-out, Commander,' said Morrow tightly. 'I doubt if you could find a piece big enough to hold in two hands. And Barker was good! The best! I just don't understand it!'

He glared at Kano.

'It's the computer! We all saw the orbital velocity

and the rate of descent. No ship could stand up to the G-factors the onboard computer sent us. If Irving or Barker hadn't been ordered to stick to the computer flight-path, they'd have seen they couldn't make it. So why did your bloody computer send them to their deaths?'

Kano's small, muscular body tensed.

'Paul!' Koenig rapped out. 'Save the adrenalin. And you, David, cool it! If there's a computer fault, it can be located. Nothing's going to bring the pilots of Eagle Six back now. We just have to be sure nothing like this occurs again. Get to it, David,' he ordered.

His gaze swept the brightly-lit deck.

'We've lost two good men. I mean to find out why.'

'How?' asked Professor Bergman.

'I want another survey Eagle to go down there.'

'No!' Morrow called out. 'You can't do it, John!'

Koenig said harshly:

'I can, and I will! But this time, the pilots use onboard systems only. Computer stays right out of the picture until we find that malfunction.'

Morrow's big face looked drawn.

'You have to let me go, John.'

'No! Send Carter and a good co-pilot.' Koenig softened his voice. 'I want you here, Paul, to monitor every stage in the flight. You will arrange a programme of fail-safes so that the pilots can cut out immediately anything goes wrong. And you will have a hook-up with fail-safe systems.'

Morrow's face was still set in grim lines, but he appreciated the safeguards Koenig had ordered.

'I'll do it, Commander,' he said. 'And the first sign of trouble, I abort the mission.'

Koenig nodded in dismissal.

'Now, Victor,' he said to Bergman, 'what do you make of the planet?'

Bergman stared at the computer read-outs, with their glowing forecast.

'You know, it all becomes a little suspect.'

'That would be my interpretation,' agreed Koenig. 'Well?'

'I'd like to know whose ruins they are. And especially what Barker saw at the tower.' Bergman crossed to the console at the big screen. 'Let's hear the last few seconds of transmission from Eagle Six,' he ordered.

Koenig heard Barker's low, insistent tones once more. The sense of loss and waste began to weigh heavily on him.

'Now,' said Bergman.

'Commander, did you see the tower? Did you see it?' came Barker's voice.

'Well?'

'He knew you'd already seen it.'

Koenig was still thinking of the moment of impact. Eagle Six would be a smoking shower of fragments, the men nothing but ash and dust.

'John, it's important,' insisted Bergman. 'He knew you'd seen the tower. The way he said it on the re-run just now meant something different.'

'So?'

'Barker wanted to see what had happened to the tower!'

Koenig nodded.

'We'll find out soon enough. Controller Morrow, have you briefed the pilots?'

'Ready now, Commander,' said Morrow.

'Then get them launched.'

The two pilots showed none of Irving and Barker's zest for the venture; but there was no reluctance in their faces either. They were professionals, accustomed to facing danger.

'Good luck,' Koenig said. 'And remember, you take no chances.'

'Yes, sir,' answered Carter. He paused for a moment. 'They were friends of mine.'

Koenig thought of the smouldering wreckage they would find. He could think of nothing to say.

Suddenly, the planet seemed much less desirable.

CHAPTER FOURTEEN

During the hours of the flight, Koenig checked and rechecked all the data so far received about the planet. The computer's forecasts were now effusively optimistic.

His doubts remained.

While he was examining the relative orbital velocities of the Moon and the mysterious planet, a report came through from Eagle Three.

'Carter here,' came the voice. The screen showed both pilots. 'We're holding our predicted course, Commander Koenig. Checks with Controller Morrow agree our readings. According to our plot, we're ready for orbital descent right above the site of the Eagle Six crash.'

'They're right down the line,' put in Morrow.

'Good work,' said Koenig. 'Carter, take the Eagle in.'

'I can give you visuals now,' said Kano. 'We're using long-range scanners right above the planet.'

'Do that,' said Koenig.

He tried not to show the inner tenseness that clawed at him. It was always the same when you had to send someone else out: you endured your fears and distilled them into a corrosive brew. It burned within you, and outwardly you had to maintain the appearance of confidence.

'Still holding well,' said Carter.

'Confirmed,' agreed Morrow.

His stubby fingers hovered over the console, which was a duplicate of the controls of the survey Eagle. Koenig saw the panic button glowing red. Morrow would abort the mission instantly if danger appeared.

'Easy,' he said quietly. 'They're not close enough yet.'

They saw the Eagle then, swooping above a belt of high cloud. Outlined against the whiteness, it looked frail. White flame gouted from its engines.

'Cutting approach speed,' reported Carter.

'It looks good,' Morrow told him. 'You're still right on line.'

'Commander Koenig, I'm relaying direct visuals from the onboard scanners,' said Carter. 'You'll see what we see from here on. Descent path *now*!'

The screen shivered with white light, and then filled with hazy blurs as the scanners tried to penetrate the cloud cover. And then there was no need, for the Eagle dived through and away from the great white banks of vapour and into bright sunlight.

'Commander!' yelled Carter. 'Eagle Three to Commander Koenig—do you see it?'

Koenig had glimpsed something.

A great black tower. The remains of buildings, half-fallen and blackened. He blinked and looked again: a skeletal shape hung above a hillside.

'It's Eagle Six!' someone yelled incredulously.

Carter's voice boomed throughout Mission Control.

'I see the ship, Commander—Eagle Six!'

Koenig couldn't believe it, but nevertheless it had been there. Carter had reported it. The crew around him had seen it. Bergman was slapping his back, Morrow was pounding the console like a maniac, and David Kano was yelling to him that two men they believed dead must be alive down on the surface of the planet.

'I get it in exactly the crash-site location!' Carter was yelling. 'I don't know what weird trick Ed Barker and Bud Irving pulled to do it, but they got the Eagle down!'

Morrow roared for confirmation.

'Repeat this, Carter! You have direct visual sighting of Eagle Six?'

'Confirmed, Controller—I see it hanging nose-down just a few metres above the ground. It didn't crash —they're alive!'

Bergman was frankly babbling:

'It's wonderful, John! I knew it—this is our planet. It's the end of all that space-wandering. It's going to be our home. A miracle like that is a sign to us—'

He stopped, and seemed to recollect his position as the cool intellectual whose reputation was based on emotionless cerebration:

'That is, Commander Koenig, I think we should accept computer's advice.'

Koenig frowned. There was too much elation throughout the whole of Moonbase Alpha. Yet Carter's enthusiasm was irrepressible.

'You just have to see this place, Commander! It seems so different when you get down close. Anything can happen here—'

'Carter, I want a check on your report,' he said loudly. 'First, are you in communication with Pilots Barker and Irving?'

'No, Commander.' His tone had sobered.

Koenig turned to Kano:

'Anything from Eagle Six?'

'Not a word, Commander.'

'Nothing direct to us, and nothing to Eagle Three,' said Koenig. He spoke to Carter again: 'Is Eagle Six still hovering above the planetary surface?'

'It is, Commander.'

'And have you a sighting of either pilot?'

'I guess not, Commander,' said Carter. 'No, sir.'

'And is the Eagle under power?'

'John,' said David Kano, 'it has to be under power to hold that configuration.'

'It *has* to be powered,' agreed Morrow.

'Answer, Pilot Carter!' rapped Koenig. 'Check with on-board calculators and sensor—what are the power-levels of Eagle Six!'

There was a pause of a full minute.

When Carter spoke, he was icily calm, the trained and alert Eagle pilot once more, not a man who has just found that his friends have not been uselessly killed on a strange planet.

'Eagle Six gives no power readings, Commander. I have no contact with its crew.' He waited and then said: 'Orders, Commander?'

Koenig again felt the strong sense of alarm that had filled him when Barker and Irving had begun their crazy death-dive. There was a brooding eerie quality about the planet, an almost hypnotic deadliness. He shivered. It was as though tiny claws were driving deep into his mind. And he knew that it all centred on the rearing black tower.

He looked about the circle of men and women in Main Mission Control. He was surprised to see that they did not share his pessimism. If anything, the atmosphere had changed to one of complacency. Yet they were aware of his uncertainty.

He turned to the big screen.

'Here are your orders, Carter. Remain on observation near Eagle Six. On no account land on the surface. Understood?'

The landscape of the planet faded. In its place came the sharply delineated forward deck of the survey Eagle. Carter was taking off his helmet.

'Now, Commander, why be so uptight? One little look isn't going to harm anyone—'

'They've landed!' Koenig exclaimed. 'Controller Morrow, get that ship up!'

Morrow was smiling in an inane way. Koenig saw the same fatuous smile on Carter's face.

'Now, John,' cautioned Morrow, placing a meaty hand on Koenig's shoulders. 'Take it easy! I knew they were going down—'

'Carter, get that ship into orbit!' roared Koenig. He pushed Morrow aside, and for all his size and strength the big Controller found himself moving fast away from the console. Koenig began to press buttons to get the Eagle into the blue sky of the strange planet.

Morrow was laughing. So was Kano. And Bergman.

Others joined in. There was a zany, indulgent good humour in their laughter. A fat technician doubled up over his console, holding his stomach against the pain of his jerking laughter.

'Oh, John,' boomed Morrow, 'don't bother—I've taken the monitors off. I had to give them a chance to see for themselves. Now wasn't that fair?'

He was still chuckling as he returned to the console. He didn't seem to resent the rough treatment he had received.

Koenig shook his head. Suddenly, he was in the midst of a crew of madmen. Anger rose up, but Professor Bergman spoke before he could try to bring the Alphans back to their senses.

'John, Piri will be your home too.'

The words had an instantly calming effect, not only on Koenig himself, but on the laughing men and women in Main Mission Control. The fat technician sat down, still weak, but attentive. Koenig listened to Bergman with disbelief.

'I think it would be an excellent plan for us all to go down to Piri, John. It is a most delightful place. I don't wonder that the Eagle crews were anxious to be the first settlers. Neither they nor any of us can see any reason to remain on this tiresome satellite longer than we must.'

Bergman's ascetic features glowed. He had an air of fanatical enthusiasm that sent alarm bells ringing in Koenig's mind. The words were altogether alien to a man of Bergman's calibre. He sounded like a glib child who has learned his lesson well.

'Isn't it marvellous, John?'

Helena Russell's beautiful blue eyes stared up at him. He was astonished to see the longing in them.

'You too, Helena? But how has it happened? I gave orders to Morrow and Carter, and they've both disobeyed.' He looked about him. The Security men had the same look of infatuated delight. Clearly they would not arrest anyone.

Helena Russell took his hand.

'This is such a wretched place for real people like you and me, John. Can't you see that Piri is waiting for us? Look at it!'

Koenig looked.

The scanners were ranging closer now. They showed a beautiful landscape. No dust, no ash, no blackened rocks. In the distance, the tower was a great black sentinel. Peace and beauty, thought Koenig.

'Well, Commander?' asked Kano.

'Yes,' Koenig said, to his own amazement. 'Yes, of course!'

Koenig appreciated the wonder of it all. Men and women smiled and nodded approval. Bergman waved to the screen as if making a marvellously philanthropic gesture. He seemed to be giving the planet to Koenig. Of course Victor was right about Piri, thought Koenig. What a fool he had been not to see it right away!

'The best of climates and vegetation,' Kano assured him. 'Computer says so!'

'Computer?' said Koenig slowly.

Bergman smiled reassuringly:

'Now, John, you've had more strain than any of us—but on Piri, that will all be over!'

'We'll be happy,' whispered Helena.

'It's made for us,' agreed Bergman.

Koenig felt slightly embarrassed. Helena was trying to nuzzle against him, whilst Morrow was beaming approval. If only the stray, needling doubts would go!

He repeated Bergman's phrase:

'It's made for us? *Made* for us?'

And the alarm-bells shrilled.

'Victor,' said Koenig slowly, 'how do you know the planet is called Piri?'

Bergman patted him on the back, as if remonstrating with an amiable drunk.

'But what else *should* a planet like Piri be called? Piri *is* Piri—the planet of peace.'

He smiled benevolently.

And Koenig knew it was true.

'Yes, Victor,' he said. 'Yes, of course.'

'Then that's settled, John,' said Bergman briskly.

Kano looked about him.

'This is one place I don't want to see again!'

'We can leave the rocks and the dust,' said Helena, like a housewife contemplating a spring-cleaning. 'John, I can't wait to get to Piri!'

Morrow slapped Kano on the back.

'And I said the computer was wrong—David, I guess an apology is overdue!'

Kano grinned back in the inane way Koenig was beginning to detest.

'Forget it, Paul! When we get down to Piri, we'll pension off the computer. No more Eagles, no more astro-navigation, no more servicing these systems—and am I looking forward to it!'

Koenig shared momentarily in the pleasurable comtemplation of a future on Piri. And still a tiny edge of doubt clawed at his mind. There had been no word from Baker and Irving. Neither of the two men had been sighted by the crew of the second survey Eagle. They hadn't explained the weird way in which their Eagle hung poised over the surface of the planet. And could there be an explanation for it?

Yet there were most glowing reports from all sources now. The onboard calculators and sensors confirmed computer's interpretations of readings: *Piri* was a wonderfully suitable planet for the tired Alphans. Promise, and mystery.

Koenig said:

'It's remarkable, Victor. But can we rely on the computer read-outs? They were at variance with the time-schedules of the Eagle we sent out first—'

Morrow laughed aloud:

'John, I guess that Zenno experience left you sour—can't you believe we've hit the jackpot?'

'The evidence is right in front of you,' Kano put in. 'Visuals from Moonbase scanners, confirmed visuals from Eagle three, read-outs from all computers, and direct reports from the Eagle survey crew!'

'We're getting requests from all Sections for passage down to Piri,' Bergman said. 'Who can blame them?'

'We are?' asked Koenig, bewildered now.

Helena Russell joined in: 'On medical grounds I

think that we should authorize an extended excursion to Piri. We need to breathe air and be free of machines! Don't you feel that, John?'

Koenig did. Every fibre of his being responded to the dream of a stress-free existence on the idyllic planet. And still he hesitated:

'There has been life on Piri before we arrived. The tower artifacts prove it—'

'But not malevolent life, John!' burst out Bergman. 'I can see that only a benign and humane intelligence created the tower of Piri.'

'We have no choice, John,' said Morrow. '*You* have no choice!'

Koenig looked about him. Quietly, scores of Alphans had entered Main Mission Control. All had the flushed, hectic excitement that Morrow showed. Kcenig sensed the massed willpower.

'John, it is what we wish,' said Helena Russell, in the tone he knew from an earlier time, when he lay between life and death after the crash of the exploratory Eagle at the huge crater. 'We need Piri. And so do you.'

Koenig felt himself in agreement. They were right. Yet his words surprised even him. It seemed that another, more pessimistic, Koenig spoke:

'It is no light decision to leave the safety of Moonbase Alpha,' he said quietly but with a ring of authority which brought the Alphans to a renewed awareness of his stature amongst them. 'What we hear from the computer is what we wish to hear if our most treasured hopes were realized. But I'm not satisfied! So far, we have received no communication from the two men we thought lost. I find that curious, if not sinister.'

'But that's unimportant—' Morrow interrupted.

'Enough!' Koenig snapped. 'I am still Commander.

And when I authorize the evacuation of Moonbase Alpha, it will proceed. And not before!'

Helena Russell spoke for the Alphans:

'And when will that be, Commander?'

'When I send you my personal report on the planet of Piri!' Koenig turned to Morrow. In a voice like a whiplash, he said:

'Kano will accompany me. Everyone else stays. There will be no further launches until I give the word. Is that understood?'

Morrow looked mutinous. There were growls from several men, and a shrill, rising inflection of complaint from a group of female technicians. Koenig straightened. His eyes held Morrow's. Seconds passed. A full minute.

'Understood, Commander,' said Morrow at last. There was no further disagreement.

'See that the crew returns to stations, Paul,' said Koenig. Quietly, he added: 'When the Alphans leave Moonbase Alpha, it must be of their own free choice, not because computer tells them to go.'

Morrow nodded. 'Yes, Sir.'

CHAPTER FIFTEEN

Koenig stepped out on to the cold, dead world, grey and bleak. In the distance were the ruins, and the eerie black tower. After all, the green world was a traitor. The reality was as harsh as the Moon's surface.

'Wait,' he told Kano.

'But the air's fine, John. Take precautions by all means, but let's not get uptight over it.'

Koenig checked the meter he held in his hand.

'It's breathable,' he said reluctantly. 'But it all feels *wrong*.'

Kano pointed to the distant looming tower.

'Maybe we should look around. Let's move the Eagle in closer.'

'No,' said Koenig. 'Two Eagles went near the tower and the crews are missing. You stay with the Eagle while I investigate.'

Kano signed. 'Piri answers all our needs—the computer's got it right, John. But if you want to confirm the reports . . .'

'Stay with the ship.'

'Yes, Commander!'

It was unlike the Technical chief to smile in that cool and slightly mocking way, and yet Koenig had to admit that Kano had every justification. The planet was no pleasuredome, but it could sustain life, given hard work and time.

So why was he so cautious?

Koenig stepped forward and walked quickly towards the towering rock and its crumbling ruins. A curious kind of joy drifted through his entire body, almost a tingling of delighted anticipation. And then his boots crunched on fibrous root.

Koenig looked down. He unclipped the organitron from his belt and put it to the root.

The gauge hadn't altered. The root was quite dead. What life had Piri once held? Why were all the Aphans so sure the planet was beautiful, when the reality was this? Koenig looked at the top of the black tower just as a jagged wave of light sprang from its summit.

Koenig's hands went to his eyes. The black tower shimmered and seemed as if it might split. Yet there was no physical discomfort. The shock-wave of light enveloped him and then passed, but it left him comforted. Koenig again felt the sense of impending delight that had begun to spread throughout his body when he trod on the dead root. He looked towards the tower once more.

It was pulsing with shards of light. Piri was alive. Koenig was not surprised to see a girl advancing towards him. She was radiant, a young girl with the delicate skin and slender roundness of later adolescence.

'Welcome to Piri,' she said.

Koenig was stunned, not by her freshness and beauty nor by the suddenness of her appearance: it was the tremendous feeling of well-being that left him dazed.

She walked towards him, loose robe open so that he saw the rosebud nipples. She kissed him on the lips. It was a rebirth. All the bitterness of loss and regret ebbed away. All doubts vanished.

'Piri the beautiful,' he said. 'Piri the end of our voyaging.'

He looked about him and saw that the planet was reborn too. He was standing, not on gritsand, but amongst meadow flowers. The green of the land was painfully beautiful.

'This is where you settle, John,' she assured him. 'It is the wish of the Guardian that you are released from your suffering.' She indicated the shining tower.

'It depends on your viewpoint, I suppose,' Koenig heard himself saying. 'Bergman was right. So was Paul Morrow. And how David Kano must have laughed when I didn't believe him!'

'But now you see Piri as it is,' agreed the girl. 'Now you know the purpose of our planet. The Guardian has spread his light over you.'

Koenig looked about him. The planet was a garden.

Everywhere he looked, there were bright flowers, trees dripping with fruit, small streams sparkling under bright sunlight. Koenig shook his head, still suffering from the shock of revelation that had come with the flow of light from the tower.

'I can't believe it!' he said. 'It's an idyllic world.'

'It was meant to be,' said the girl. 'Millennia ago this planet was designed by men and women with imagination and the technical skills to realize their dreams. They built machines to regulate all life on Piri. And then there was no further need for decision, for the machines in their turn created the Guardian. Life was perfect. Even time stopped. *See!*'

She led him by the hand to a small hill. Beyond was the great tower. And there was Eagle Six, just as Carter had described it: poised in its last flight.

Koenig shook his head. A shred of disbelief remained. 'The Eagles can't hold that configuration!'

Nose down, the slender, elegant ship held position a few metres above the ground. Koenig looked away and saw Carter's Eagle, at rest in a grove of citrus trees.

'It's true,' said the Pirian girl. 'For you, the Guardian has suspended time. In a perfect world, time must hold still, for time brings change and change is imperfection. See, your crewmen have made their choice.'

She pointed to a flower garden.

'My men!' Koenig shouted, running. 'Carter! Barker!—'

The Pirian girl ran with him, easily, leisurely, her robe flowing with the disturbance of air. She laughed, and the garden seemed further away. None of the men appeared to notice Koenig. He stopped. It took him some time to regain his breath.

'What have you done to my men?'

'Not me, John!—the Guardian. The Guardian has allowed them to enter a new form of life.'

Koenig grasped at the almost-forgotten reason for his lack of trust in the bewitching girl.

'But when Kano and I landed, I saw only gritsand and dead hills. The tower was black and ruined. And I found this!' Koenig said, holding out the grey root.

'The Guardian has ordained that Piri should live again for you,' the girl said. 'John, I was sent to check your doubts. Believe me, this is your home. It is the place of peace at last.'

Koenig shook his head: 'I want my men.'

'They are at peace, John.'

'The peace of death!' Koenig roared. He knew that the Zennites had given him the ability to see into the nature of reality in a way that was not shared by the Alphans. He could resist the spell of Piri.

'I'm taking my men back!'

'No,' said the girl. 'The Guardian will make you perfect too!'

She put a hand to his arm. It was a grip of steel. Her wide-set eyes stared into his and he shivered, for there was no spark of humanity, no exchange of emotion. Koenig pulled away. His arm was numb from the effort. And then he ran back towards Kano and the Eagle.

Kano ran to meet him.

'Kano, get back to the ship!' Koenig panted. 'Lift off immediately!'

Kano was aghast. 'But, John, the Guardian has given us the prime directive! We are to stay on—'

Koenig's mind reeled. Kano knew that the Guardian existed! He pushed past him, making for the open port.

'John, come back!'

He too gripped Koenig, but he had not the numbing

power of the Pirian girl. Koenig easily twisted free. Kano leapt at him, his face full of a terrifying pity.

'John, we have to keep you—'

There was an attempt at a cunning hold, but Koenig had heard enough. He bunched his fist and crashed it into Kano's face. The man spun away, still pleading, but he was far from finished. He leapt like a cat, his face streaming blood. A boot lashed into Koenig's side. Ribs cracked. Then Kano's hand chopped like an axe. If it had landed as Kano intended, Koenig's arm would have broken. But Koenig had reached the port. He kicked back and felt his boot land in Kano's unprotected belly.

Kano fell back then. He was still trying to plead with him, Koenig realized. There was a look of trust, affection and despair in his dark eyes. He wanted to save his Commander from the suffering of Moonbase Alpha.

Koenig punched commands, and the Eagle rose fast into the strange dark sky. He looked down once and thought he saw cold dark hills stretching into the far distance. The pain from his side made him retch.

'Commander to Moonbase,' he said as a great tide of blackness rushed towards him. 'Take over guidance of the Eagle. I am incapacitated and . . .'

He didn't hear the answer from Bergman: 'John? This is Victor. How come you got hurt down on Piri? The Guardian surely wouldn't allow trouble? Get back soon, John—we'll save you a glass of champagne!'

Koenig staggered into Main Mission Control when the party was in full swing.

'John!' boomed Paul Morrow. 'You made it!'

Koenig's senses reeled. No one seemed to have noticed his condition. Blood still streamed from his face. He clutched his side in agony, yet none of the

Alphans seemed in the least concerned that he was hurt and exhausted.

Morrow came across: 'Here's to our very own Christopher Columbus—the founder of our New World!'

Koenig knew Morrow would slap him on the back. He couldn't halt the affectionate blow, nor move fast enough to avoid it.

'John Koenig!' roared the Alphans in approval, their faces alight with the kind of awed wonder Koenig had seen on the faces of Carter and the other Eagle pilots.

Morrow's hand came down, and Koenig pitched into agonized blackness.

CHAPTER SIXTEEN

A reedy electronics voice awoke Koenig.

'Section G Seven will complete loading on schedule at 0958 Lunar Time.'

Koenig knew he was hurt. He felt his side. His broken ribs had been strapped. Helena Russell had been at the party. Had she doctored him?

The party! It had been a celebration in his honour. The Alphans had acclaimed him as their personal deliverer. Koenig threw back the covers. A medical orderly hurried across.

'Commander, you should be moved by trolley.'

'Moved? Moved where?'

'Why, sir, to the scheduled Eagle.' The orderly

was used to the after-effects of shock. 'Commander, you won't be left behind. Don't worry, sir. Dr Russell has personally arranged your transportation.'

Koenig got his feet to the floor.

'Stay in bed, sir!'

'Tell me why I'm being moved to the Eagle!'

'Why, to ferry down to Piri, Commander,' the man said. It was clear that Commander Koenig's accident had left him with a degree of amnesia. Koenig glared back.

'No one goes to Piri!'

'Eagle Two-Six will lift off from Launch Pad One, taking up parking position on planetary surface as co-ordinates scheduled by the Guardian,' reported the reedy electronic voice. 'All Alphans in Section D-three prepare for evacuation in twenty minutes.'

'Soon be our turn, Commander,' said the orderly soothingly, yet with an excited, anticipatory glitter in his eyes. 'Why don't you relax?'

Koenig recognized the man's excitement now. The orderly—like the rest of the Alphans—was in the grip of Piri's hypnotic powers.

'John!' called Helena Russell. 'You're too ill to be on your feet—get back into bed!'

Koenig motioned the orderly to leave them.

'Helena, you too?' he said, realizing that it was so.

'If you don't lie down, John Koenig, I'll give you a knock-out jab,' she warned. She smiled delightedly. 'Though I don't know . . . When we're down on Piri, you'll soon get fit. Just don't exert yourself too much.'

Koenig took her slim hand. She looked down and smiled again, this time as if acknowledging a possibility.

'John! Can't it wait till we get to Piri?'

'Helena, do I look as though I'm crazy?' asked Koenig steadily.

'No, John!' she said, still kittenish. 'I wondered if we'd ever—'

'I'm not talking about you and me! I mean, do you think I am in a fit mental state to tell you about the real Piri—what it *is*?'

'Of course, John—but we've had your reports already. And very explicit they were.'

'You've had reports from me?'

She smiled indulgently at him.

'Yes!'

'And I said that Piri is gritsand and dead ruins?'

'Now you are talking crazy, John! Why, your report confirmed everything David Kano said about the planet. *And* what Carter and the other Eagle crew reported in.'

'They've sent in reports?'

'Of course! Everything's been checked by computer, John. And computer's not only recommended evacuation of Moonbase Alpha, its organized a schedule for evacuation: Operation Exodus.'

It wasn't just the crewmen who were deceived by Piri's strange glamour. Highly trained, intelligent men and women believed in the Guardian's evil benevolence. Koenig felt cold. But he smiled back, as if he had been reassured.

'Then that's settled,' he said. 'I'll check with Victor about securing Moonbase Alpha. I'd like to see computer's programme for preservation.'

'But we'll never need Moonbase Alpha again!'

Koenig got to his feet. 'It'll make an interesting museum-piece for future generations. Let me have my way, Helena?'

She smiled and shook her head. Cautious to the last, that was John Koenig. Why couldn't he let the Guardian worry about the future?

Main Mission Control was quiet, except for the occasional announcements of Eagle departures. The evacuation was progressing in an orderly fashion. Professor Bergman and Paul Morrow glanced up from the computer console as Koenig walked unsteadily across the dull black floor.

'John! You should be in bed!' said Bergman. Morrow joined in the concern for his welfare.

'Thanks, I'm feeling better. Look, Victor, may I see the computer read-outs of my reports?'

'But why?' said Morrow. 'You'll be going down to Piri for good soon. John, don't *worry* so much!'

'Let the Guardian do the worrying now,' said Bergman. 'Relax! Take life easier—it's the prime directive from now on.'

That phrase again: *the prime directive.* Koenig remembered Kano using it. A directive was an instruction. It was the Guardian's command: relax, sleep, stop time, *die!* Yet how could he get Bergman to believe it?

He tried reason.

'Victor,' he said. 'Just look at these read-outs.'

'Well, John?'

Morrow busied himself monitoring the plans for the evacuation of the nuclear generating areas, the heart of Moonbase.

'Victor, I reported that Piri was a dead planet. The organitron showed no sign of life. There has been no living thing on Piri for millennia.' Bergman stared back fixedly. He didn't seem to have heard. Koenig went on, faster: 'My orders were that we should not rely on computer. I believe it has been taken over by the Pirian machines that produced the Guardian. Victor, computer has been feeding us bogus information.'

Bergman nodded. 'Sure, John. You're right to stay sceptical. It wouldn't be right to have a Garden of

Eden without a doubter. But the Guardian will set your mind at rest. It's the most civilized entity I could imagine.'

'Civilized?' Koenig shouted. 'There's a kind of civilization down there, but it's one that reduces us to mindless apathy! Can't you understand that there's no such thing as perfection for us, Victor? Once we think that, we're finished! Men aren't docile! They're not tractable! Victor, we're born to struggle, and once we lose the will to fight, we all die!'

'Ah, John,' said Helena behind him. He had not heard her enter Main Mission Control. 'You're still getting memory-blank-offs from the crash at the crater. I think you should go into hypno-sleep until Operation Exodus is concluded. Just hold still, John.'

'No!' Koenig roared.

Morrow was moving towards him purposefully. And Morrow had the build of an ox. Koenig blindly staggered away. Under the anaesthetizing strappings, his ribs creaked painfully.

'No, leave him, Paul!' Bergman told Morrow. 'And you, Helena, let him have his way. He'll come to his senses soon. John,' he said to Koenig, and he might have been a kindly father allowing a child to rebel and thus find his true strengths. 'John, no one thinks you're crazy.'

Koenig halted. In a situation like this, he must use every advantage offered. The three Alphans were willing to let him hold on to what they thought were his fantasies. He fingered the dead root which was his principal contact with the realities of dead Piri. Would it convince them too that Piri was an evil mirage?

'Well, John, what is it you want to do?' asked Bergman. Koenig hesitated. He pushed the root into his pocket. They would not accept it as anything more than a delusion on his part. Helena would probably give him the knock-out jab at once. Instead, he held out the computer read-outs:

'I want to check the computer's memory-banks directly to see if they agree with the reports from the auxiliary computers aboard the Eagles that went to Piri.'

Bergman was unimpressed, though he was determined to be fair:

'Then you should go ahead, John. If it will clear your mind, my advice is to do just that. Eh, Helena?'

'Reassurance therapy,' agreed Helena Russell. 'I suppose anyone who's gone through what he has in the past months needs to be sure. But don't be too long about it, John?'

They watched him enter the humming, dim-lit area which was Kano's preserve. The memory-banks of the computer filled the huge space. There was little sign that the computer was functioning, but Koenig knew that billion upon billion of impulses raced through each grey unit every second. Without the computer, the survival of Moonbase Alpha was problematical. With computer subverted by the technology of the ancient Pirians, the survival of the Alphans themselves was in danger.

He was glad he had not shown them the dead root.

Bergman waited until the door of the computer memory store slid silently into place.

'It's my opinion that we should complete the evacuation now!' he said. 'John can be left for a while to get rid of his doubts. A few days of solitude and reflection should do the trick.'

Morrow questioned Helena Russell with a look. She shrugged: 'John's quite capable of looking after himself. Diagnostic Unit will provide emergency treatment until he follows us. Yes, leave him, Victor.'

Her eyes were shining.

Koenig made for the auxiliary console, which could be operated manually.

'Voice-to-voice contact,' he ordered, punching in a programme.

'You have it, Commander,' a thin electronic voice told him.

'I want an evaluation of the facts I present now. First, analyse this root. He placed it in a hopper. 'Second, estimate life-expectancy for Alphans on the planet Piri. Third, evaluate your own motivation.'

The root lay undisturbed. Koenig waited impatiently.

'Analyse this root!' he repeated.

'Regrets, Commander. This system has no facilities for analysis. In answer to your second question, I refer you to the computer. As for the third—'

'Stop!'

'—Yes, Commander.' The machine waited.

'You said, "I refer you to the computer"?'

'Affirmative, Commander.'

'Then what am I talking to?'

'This is a low-grade auxiliary system, Commander.'

Koenig dreaded the answer to his next question, but nevertheless he had to ask it:

'Where is computer control now?'

'Computer control has removed to Piri, Commander.'

Koenig let his breath out slowly. It was part of a consistent pattern. Infiltration, then a complete take-over.

Aloud, he said: 'So if I want the answers, I have to go down to Piri for them.'

'That is your choice, Commander.'

Koenig picked up a heavy steel chair and threw it at the auxiliary console. It ricocheted noisily the length of the huge room. He accomplished nothing but an aggravation of his chest injuries. The auxiliary did not comment on his violent action.

When he returned to Main Mission Control, he knew that the Moonbase Alpha was deserted. He crossed to the forward con and looked out. The remaining Eagles were streaming toward Piri in a perfect formation. Koenig put his hands to his head. He was the last free Alphan.

'You need rest, John Koenig,' a sweet voice declared.

Koenig knew her.

'Sleep!' the Pirian girl said.

It would be his last sleep, Koenig knew. He had to keep awake.

CHAPTER SEVENTEEN

He kept awake by using stimulants.

The first day he spent his time trying to hook the computer's ancillary systems into a net. The low-grade calculators remained in their metal cabinets, but the directing intelligence had gone.

'I want an analytical system capable of discovering ways to run this Base,' he told the machines.

They took some time to digest the information.

'More data needed, Commander,' a reedy electronic voice told him. 'This is a directive for computer, sir.'

Lying, treacherous computer, thought Koenig. But, again, how could it be? A machine could no more tell a lie than utter a thought or hold an opinion. It had done exactly what was required of it: given data, it calculated; and, confronted by a superior machine, it had obeyed.

And the Guardian was infinitely superior.

Koenig gave up the attempts after a twenty-hour slog. He left a network of trailing leads and shattered circuits. It would need someone of the calibre of David Kano to make a computer out of the machines.

The second day passed more slowly.

Koenig deliberately forced himself to check the navigational equipment of Moonbase Alpha. It was an intellectual exercise only, yet one he could enjoy. He had a talent for astral navigation second only to that of Paul Morrow. It was mathematical drudgery, but it kept his mind clear of the subtle infection from the planet below.

If he should sleep, he would dream of peace and the deadly green of Piri. One last, long, endless sleep . . .

She came the second day, glowing with delight and sympathy.

'John Koenig, you're wrecking your health! And in such useless pursuits! No one man could put together a computer in the time you have left. But I truly admire your determination, as does the Guardian, John. The Guardian will give you your reward—you will be the leader of your people once more, but in a finer life! Come, John!'

Koenig swallowed tablets and resumed the delicate work of aligning the star-ranging scanners. Then, he could ignore her.

She was more subtle the next time.

Koenig had revised a list of maintenance schedules for the orbital scanners when she stepped delicately into the forward con of Main Mission Control.

'Just how long do you think you can resist the Guardian?' she asked. 'Another day?' She inspected his haggard face, Koenig resisted the temptation to drive his fist into the sweet face. 'Two more days? Give it up, John. Please? Your friends want it too. You see, in your weakened state, you'll soon begin hallucinating, and it will take a good deal of careful medication to get you back to normal. And if you leave it too long . . .'

'Please go,' said Koenig levelly.

The thought of the lotus-life on Piri had never seemed so attractive. And wasn't it man's dream from earliest times? There had been a hero of antiquity who had discovered just such a way of life . . . Who was he?

'No more tablets, John Koenig,' said the girl. 'You're using a dream-state to blot out the reality of Piri. Why not choose the Pirian way? Your friends have—look at them, John!'

She had been programmed well, thought Koenig. The hours of isolation in the echoing complex of Moonbase Alpha were undermining his will. The tablets did no more than induce a waking coma, as the girl had said; the real danger was the lack of human contact.

Koenig had often been an outsider. It was the nature of a commander's function, the aloneness. Yet he had never kept himself isolated from human interchange and contact. He found himself yearning for the small rewards of civilized exchanges. Bergman's sometimes irritating pontifications and his shining intellect. Kano's delight in solving problems. Morrow's big-framed clumsiness. And Helena Russell's promise of another kind of release from the loneliness.

'Your friends, John,' the girl said softly.

Koenig had to look.

The big screen glowed into life. Piri's green rolling hills gave way to closer images. Helena Russell looked around and waved gaily. Bergman looked more relaxed than Koenig had ever seen him. They were seated at an ornate table, with glasses of amber liquid before them. They wore the long, flowing robes of the Pirian girl. Slightly bronzed and fit-looking, they both joined in the gestures of invitation.

Yet both had the slightly manic gleam of excitement that had manifested itself when the second Eagle survey vessel had begun its descent. Bergman and Helena exhibited an odd absence of emotion in their eyes. It shocked Koenig to see that blankness.

The girl smiled at him:

'They are relaxed, John. The struggle is over. There can be a Paradise—it isn't a fallacious human dream. Join them!'

Koenig closed his eyes and felt the tiredness seeping through him. The drugs fought back, but the insidious sweetness of surrender began to defeat the chemicals. He felt panic give way to the peace of resignation. Arguments coasted through his mind. Why struggle against the inevitable? Why not admit that it was the ambition of the human race to do what the ancient Pirians had done—to leave control to an all-powerful machine?

'You are learning, John!' the girl cried. 'Yes, why not accept the Guardian's kindness?'

He could not.

One fragment of insight remained. It was his gift from the incomparable Vana. She had taken him beyond the fabric of the immortal city of the Zennites and shown him the difference between reality and dream—intermixed though they were, there was a point where falseness began. And it was here, right here in the evil glamour of the girl, the messenger of the Guardian!

'Get out!' Koenig roared. 'Out!'

He found he was sobbing for breath. The struggle had drained him. A memory came back, one that had almost vanished from his thoughts. Zenno's strange shadowy purple towers hung before him, their pinnacles soaring into the deep purple of the night sky. He could almost see through them to the ethereal fabric of which they were composed.

Almost, he could begin to build with the Zennites.

He knew afresh what he had lost when he made his choice. When the Pirian girl came on the third day of his lonely vigil, he found fresh strength from the knowledge of what he had given up on Zenno.

'Look,' Koenig said to the blank-eyed girl, 'why *us?* I know that we of Moonbase Alpha have been seduced by the machine you call the Guardian, but why take us—a race that cannot begin to compare in sophistication with the Pirians?'

She might have been a machine herself, for she spoke without looking at him in a toneless voice: 'By your presence in the space between the stars, you have violated the peace of ancient Piri!'

'But we didn't set the course! Our satellite is out of control! We can only go where the Moon takes us!'

He could argue now, fight if he had to.

'But,' she said, and her voice was sweet as honey now, 'we have to make you perfect so that you are fit for life on the planet of peace! That is the Guardian's directive, John.'

'So you admit it—your machine, this Guardian as you call it, sabotaged our computer and misled the Alphans into believing that Piri is a paradise?'

'The Guardian gave instructions, John,' she said.
'They were obeyed by your primitive installations.
It is right and proper that you should be brought
to an understanding of the peace of Piri.'

'The peace of Piri! But what happened to all the
happy and contented Pirians? Where are they now?'

'The Guardian gave them rest.'

'But *where are they*!'

She smiled as sweet as death. Her lips were moist
with a dew that sparkled. Vibrant and beautiful, she
was venomous to Koenig.

'The Guardian changed the Pirians.'

'Just as we shall be changed!'

'John,' the girl said, and her tender smile mocked
him by its youthful charm. 'Come, John, Helena is
waiting.'

Koenig groped for tablets. Three days without sleep.
How much longer could he last? There were limits
to a normal man's bodily endurance. Freaks could
manage without sleep; but the ordinary metabolism
of a human body demanded regular deep sleep. Soon,
the demands of the body would resist the drugs.

'Helena is asking for you, John!'

As she said it, he thought of the mature beauty
of the woman. Helena Russell's brilliant blue eyes
swam before him and he stumbled. The girl waited.
Koenig grazed his knee against the console and the
pain brought him back to full consciousness.

'No!' he gasped. 'No!'

'Come, John! Peace—rest and peace!'

'The peace of death!'

'Not for you and Helena, John.'

Helena. Koenig clung to the thought. He had been
saved once before by a woman. *Helena*—what had
she done for him in the past?

'John?' whispered the girl, sure now of him.

Koenig closed his mind. He blinked against the

brilliant light of the empty deck. Helena—she had placed something over his heart. She had persisted when others might have abandoned him. There had been the brief agony of shock . . .

Koenig clamped down firmly on the rest of the memory. In some weird way, the machines of the planet below could affect the human mind with apparent ease. They may or may not have the ability to read his mind; he would take no chances. He looked down to the console, where a mathematical conundrum remained to be solved. He concentrated on the problems of astro-navigation.

Some time later, he looked up.

The girl was still there, still with that tender concerned smile in place. She seemed to suspect nothing.

'You are ready, John?' she asked.

'I am ready.'

'The Eagle is waiting.'

'The last of the Eagles.'

'You will see your Alphans again. All of them. A completely new existence will be yours. All this primitive technology is now a thing of the past for you, John. Your Moon will stay in orbit around Piri, but you will forget—'

Koenig could not help his exclamation:

'The Moon in orbit! Held here! But we'll never be able to get away!'

'Nor will you wish to, John.'

Koenig gritted his teeth. Now, more than ever, he must control himself and his thoughts. The Guardian had taken his crew, his ships and the base. Now, the Moon hung against the threat of the Guardian's power.

And what could he do? The Guardian held all power sources, controlled all the decision-making apparatus of Moonbase Alpha. Despite himself, Koenig smiled at the thought. Whilst there was one man who could endure against the mind-bending deceptions of the Pirians' machines, there was hope. And there were power supplies . . .

'I shall bring a few small souvenirs with me,' he told the watching girl.

'They are not necessary.'

'Nevertheless I shall bring them.'

'If it pleases you. The Guardian will have no objections, John.'

Koenig spent a few minutes selecting the equipment he needed. The girl waited patiently. As he emerged from the Diagnostic Unit, she took his hand. Koenig shuddered. He felt like a tame animal reclaimed by its indulgent owner.

He checked the standard survival kit of his spacesuit at Flight Control. The huge deck echoed to the tramp of his metalled feet. Grotesquely large in the spacesuit, he watched his long shadow approach the last of the Eagles. The girl walked by his side, diaphanous robes swirling.

Koenig felt for the butt of the stun-gun. Its comforting bulk nestled in his hand.

It wasn't much against the mysterious might of the Guardian of Piri.

'Commander Koenig requesting flight-path to Piri,' he said to the onboard computer console.

'The Guardian has arranged co-ordinates, Commander,' the thin electronic voice assured him.

Koenig smiled grimly.

'I expected no less.'

He settled to watch the planet take shape before him once more.

CHAPTER EIGHTEEN

The strange spell was lifted. When Koenig stepped from the Eagle, it was on to a dead world. For as far as he could see, there were only grey-black hills and drifting sands. It was a landscape to send a chill through the soul.

'Now you can become one with your comrades, John,' said the blank-eyed girl. She pointed to the tower. 'You must accept willingly the dominion of the Guardian, as your comrades have done.'

Koenig let the space-armour slide to the grey sand. He retained the small pack and the stun-gun. The girl didn't seem to notice. Her strange eyes were fixed on the enigmatic tower that dominated the low blackened hills. Coarse gritsand crunched under Koenig's boots.

'I'm ready,' he said. There was only the shadow of a plan. He strode beside the girl with fear beginning to gnaw at his mind.

Only when Koenig was near the tower was the insidious radiation from the Pirian's machines strong enough to overcome his Zennite powers. One moment the tower was grim and black, a great tombstone to the memory of the Pirians, and then it became a radiant white beacon, an invitation to a new life.

Koenig guarded his eyes from the glare. He looked down and saw a small valley between gently-sloping hills. Trees and flowers and tiny streams made a hauntingly beautiful scene. Fruit hung heavy on bushes and trees; it was no wonder that the Alphans had been dazed by their good fortune. Piri idealized their deepest longings.

'See!' the girl announced.

All the Alphans were there, bronzed and fit. All attired in the robes of the Pirians. All with the blank-eyed stare and inane grin Koenig loathed. Helena Russell ran to him, her long blonde hair streaming in the wind.

'John, you finally made it!'

The other Alphans ostentatiously turned away, glad for him, and willing to allow him some privacy now that he too shared their wonderful secret. Koenig held the slender body in his arms. He looked over Helena's head as she moulded herself against him. Bergman's pale face was almost rubicund. Morrow held a bunch of grapes high and pressed them in his big hands. The purple juice ran on to his big nose and trickled into his mouth. He laughed at the pleasure of it.

Koenig smiled his greetings to them. They waved and returned to the dalliance of Piri, their faces bewildered by happiness. Koenig stroked the fine blonde hair:

'Helena, come with me,' he said.

The deceiving words were difficult to say. Dr Helena Russell was a colleague, a friend, and a loved one. He was about to betray her. But the words had to be said. He had to convince at least one of the Alphans that the lotus fruits were deadly.

'Come with you, John? What else? You only had to crook your finger,' she murmured. Her robe was open to the waist. She smiled as he looked down at her well-shaped breasts. 'I've waited so long for this, John!' she sighed. She held him possessively.

'This way, Helena.'

They walked away, arms around one another to the shade of a fruit-heavy tree. Koenig looked back. The Alphans were out of sight.

'I have a surprise for you, Helena.'

'John!' she said, delighted.

'Close your eyes.'

Trusting and child-like, she obeyed. It was a game. Life was constant pleasure. John had learned what Piri meant.

'It's a pendant,'said Koenig.

He took the string of wiring and the bright, flat electrodes from the pack. The apparatus wasn't unlike a piece of jewellery. It glittered in the sunlight, reflecting shards of light on the rich, dark leaves above. He arranged the discs over her heart.

'Can I open my eyes, John?'

'Not yet.'

He set up the power unit.

'Now?'

'In a moment.'

He pressed a switch. Helena shrieked. Her eyes opened, wide and blue and alive with shock and fear.

'*John!*'

Koenig could not look at her. He stepped up the charge. Her arms came up to tear the electrodes away as intelligence came to her. Her eyes glared hate when he looked at her again. Through the pain and shock she knew that she had been robbed of something infinitely precious. Recognition and understanding quickly followed.

'Take it steadily,' Koenig warned. 'Helena, do you know where you are?'

The furious denunciations died on her lips as she looked about her. Fresh shock appeared in her face. Koenig reached out a hand and took her bare shoulder. She looked down and saw that her robe was open, and a very human emotion chased across her face.

She covered her breasts. Her face was crimson. Memories were returning fast.

'The planet—we call it Piri.'

'They called it Piri.'

Helena got to her feet and looked down at the electrodes. 'You used this on me? The electrodes—they were to stimulate my heart?'

'To shock you out of whatever hypno-jag you were on.'

'The Pirians! The Guardian—is that it?'

'It was some form of mass hypnosis. You and the rest of the Alphans.'

'They invited us to share their planet,' she said, and again knew her loss. She looked about her. 'It was so beautiful. But there's only black rocks and gritsand—John, what happened to it all?'

'The planet is dead, except for machines.'

'But they were so kind, so real!'

'Shadows. Projections maybe of long-dead Pirians by the machine that calls itself the Guardian.'

'So it's over?' she said.

'Dr Russell, you were chasing a dream,' Koenig said. He watched the softness disappear from her eyes. In seconds, she had become professional again. She took the necklace of electrodes from her neck. 'You resisted the Guardian, John. How?'

'I'm not sure, but I suspect it's something to do with what happened when I was with the Zennites.' He felt a pang of regret. 'I may have absorbed some of their mind-control techniques.'

'And so the Pirian machines couldn't influence you.' She frowned. 'But all of us—even Professor Bergman—were completely deluded.'

'And I had to shake the influence of the Guardian. I remembered the old-fashioned shock-treatment you used to bring me back. Now I want to get Bergman and Morrow out of their hypnosis, then we can get to work on the rest—'

Helena Russell interrupted him:

'There isn't time!' she cried. 'We were waiting for you.' She pointed to the tower. 'The Pirians promised that we should be made perfect when you came, John.'

'Perfect!' Koenig growled. 'There's only one kind of perfection on Piri—euthanasia!'

Even now, the evil glamour of the Guardian's promises still affected Helena Russell. 'We were to become immortal,' she said longingly. 'Soon.'

Koenig thought fast. 'There were no Pirians. Except for the girl with the empty eyes. What is to happen? Did the Pirians explain?'

'There is to be a ceremony, where we dedicate ourselves to the Guardian's care. We bathe in the light from the great Tower of Piri. That is the prime directive.'

And there it was again, the odd phrase *prime directive*. It seemed to have a deep meaning for the entranced Alphans.

'When is the ceremony to take place?' Koenig snapped.

'Immediately! As soon as you joined us. The Guardian wished the peace of Piri to extend to all the Alphans at the same moment.'

Koenig looked towards the strange tower. It began to glow with the ghostly, glittering radiance he had seen before. He knew in that moment that it was the last thing the ancient Pirians had seen. If he didn't act at once, the grim infection would overcome him too. He checked the load of the stun-gun.

'Then let's not keep the Guardian waiting!'

The light from the tower was so intense that Koenig and Helena Russell had to shield their eyes. They stumbled forward and heard a chorus of delighted greeting. In the shattering glare, the Alphans stood entranced.

'We have found paradise!' Morrow yelled, and his huge face was transfigured. Koenig heard the words and had trouble associating them with the hard-headed Controller he knew. 'Lead us into the care of the Guardian, John!'

Bergman too had a maniacal exultance. 'The Guardian brings gifts, John! Peace and delight forever!'

'Commander, there will be no more pain!' called a slim girl, and Koenig recognized Eva Zoref. He glared around the yelling, awed, ecstatic throng and saw that the Guardian had improved on its projections. The Alphans stood in a garden that was breathtakingly beautiful. It was the human race's ideal of the hereafter: fountains sparkling in the eerie light, graceful statuary, brilliant flowers, fruits glistening with dew, animals and birds adding their call and colour and movement to the scene.

'See, John, it's all yours!' called the Pirian girl. 'The Peace of Piri!'

Momentarily, Koenig had trouble in locating the source of the voice. He sheltered his eyes once more and picked her out, high above him on a dais in the centre of the paradisical garden. His reaction was instant. Loathing forced a roar of protest from him:

'No! *No!* Alphans, she brings only death!'

He pushed through the crowd. They seemed to be deaf. Koenig grabbed Morrow by the arm. 'There are no Pirians—the Guardian made sure they had no more will to live!'

'Peace!' Morrow beamed back at him.

'Rest!' Bergman shrilled.

Koenig pushed through to the dais and bellowed:

'You can't condemn them like this! They're not sheep, to die for the Guardian!'

The girl turned those strange, emotionless eyes on him. Koenig felt the radiation from the tower increase. Needles of fear and horror slipped through his mind. The Guardian's terrible forces were at work.

'To me, Alphans!' Koenig bellowed. 'See, Helena Russell was hypnotized, but she got free of the Guardian!'

Helena pushed through to his side. Her lips were moving, but Koenig could not hear what she was trying to say.

He heard the Pirian girl, though:

'The Guardian gives you the Peace of Piri!'

Every one of the entranced Alphans stopped to listen. Breath held back, lest a syllable should be lost, they were as still as the dead.

'Peace,' they sighed at last.

Koenig shivered with dread. He too could glimpse the peace the Guardian offered. And Helena Russell had the look of a drowning woman.

'The Guardian has taken pain from your lives!' called the girl, and Koenig found himself unable to speak.

'We are grateful to the Guardian!' sighed the Alphans.

'The Guardian will give you perfection!'

'We shall be perfect!' came the chanted answer.

'No,' whispered Koenig, fighting to control his speech faculties once more. 'No, Bergman—don't you see—'

Again the clear, bell-like voice called out in a cry that was an incantation:

'Would you have your peace disturbed?'

'No!' the answer came, much more strongly.

'Would you have your perfection flawed?'

There was genuine fear in the answer:

'No!'

'Would you have the Peace of Piri destroyed?'

Anger made the response a frightening thing:

'No!'

'Should two of the Alphans try to break the Peace of Piri, what must be done with them?'

Koenig felt afraid. Not for his own physical safety, though that was present too; he feared that the Alphans were truly lost, for they were men and women full of a rage that was inhuman. They had been programmed to rage as if they were extensions of the evil machines of Piri.

'Don't listen!' he yelled.

'What must be done with them?' shrilled the girl.

'Destroy them!' bawled Paul Morrow, and his heavy shoulders heaved with fury.

'Cast them out!' someone roared in Koenig's face. The man bent to pick up a stone.

'They are here, in your midst!'

'Where?' screamed the demented Alphans. 'Tell us who they are!'

The glaring light confused the Alphans. When they tried to identify the intruders, they were half-blinded.

'That woman!' shrieked the stony-eyed girl from the dais. And she pointed to Helena Russell. 'That man!' Her accusing finger singled out Koenig.

Someone caught Helena Russell by the hair and bent her backwards. A woman clutched at Helena's face with taloned fingers. Koenig stepped forward and hit swiftly, twice. Man and woman slumped, their nerve-centres paralysed.

'Destroy them!' the girl shrieked. 'The Guardian commands it!'

The Alphans bayed for blood. They clutched at one another, struggling furiously to inflict harm. But their blows were unco-ordinated, and their minds dazed by their conflicting emotions. Clumsily, they sought Koenig and Helena Russell in the ghostly-lit paradise of Piri.

'John!' called Helena behind him. She had fallen, and two men were trying to kick her in the stomach. Koenig yanked out the stun-gun and pole-axed both of them. The nearest men and women sighted him, though, and suddenly there was purpose in their actions.

'This way!' roared Koenig, yanking Helena to her feet.

'Destroy Commander Koenig—kill!' the girl screamed. She did not see Koenig and Helena Russell as they bounded up the dais ahead of the roaring pack. 'Long live the Peace of Piri!' she screamed.

'Keep out of the way!' Koenig shouted to Helena. 'Stop!' he roared to the advancing men and women.

'Destroy Koenig!' the girl screamed, and still she had not turned in his direction. Behind her, the great white Tower of Piri became a glowing, incandescent rock, terrible in its majesty. The Alphans reeled from its renewed radiance.

Koenig knew his life-span could be measured in seconds. He ignored the anguish of his broken ribs and grabbed the shrieking Pirian girl.

'See what passes for life on Piri!' he roared, and he took the light figure in his hands. Bodily he raised her high above his head. His rib-cage creaked, and the half-healed bones snapped. Sweat streamed from his face. 'See!' he roared, and with the last of his strength he hurled the screaming girl at the incandescent Tower of Piri.

A huge sighing expostulation came from the crazed Alphans. The body arced out and down, and then it seemed to dive straight through the fabric of the mysterious tower. Immediately, a sharp violent detonation crashed around the bowl of hills. The glaring whiteness gave way to furious flashes of broken light. The ground shook, and the great Tower of Piri trembled.

The Alphans clung to one another for support. Koenig caught sight of Bergman's face: there was fear there, but intelligence too. Then shock-waves tumbled him to the ground. Koenig swayed.

'Eagle Six—look!' Helena Russell yelled.

Koenig looked and saw the Eagle complete its interrupted crash-dive. Time had begun again. The tower's light blazed and then faded. Koenig saw, incredulously, that the Guardian's hold was gone.

'Run!' yelled Koenig. 'Run—it's breaking up!'

The stronger spirits heard and acted. Koenig pushed and kicked the unwilling. Helena Russell helped, and then Bergman joined in. Deeply shocked though he was, he made the effort of will to adjust to the new situation.

'John, I tried to kill you!' someone was yelling.

Koenig saw David Kano at his elbow.

'Get the Alphans moving—it's over!' he roared.

Kano's dazed expression vanished. 'Yes, Commander!'

The tower began to break up as the last Alphan was bullied into movement. Great blocks of metals showered the dais. Fragments of intricate machines rained down on the gritsand and smashed against the rocks of long-dead Piri.

The Alphans stared at one another with curiosity and wonder, as if seeing one another for the first time. Eventually, they turned to Koenig for instructions.

When the ground was still and the tower a total ruin, Koenig indicated that the quiet and awed Alphans should follow him. He led them to the body of the girl he had thrown into the white light. The face was in shreds. Part of one leg had been torn loose. Beneath the skin-like covering, they saw a complex of circuitry.

'That was the last Pirian,' said Koenig quietly. 'The Pirians faded away because they made their wills over to the machines. The last and greatest of the machines remembered what the Pirians had looked like and created this robot to beguile us.'

'So it's finished for us?' Morrow said. 'See—the Moon's held in orbit!'

The Alphans looked up at the glittering Moon. Suddenly, it seemed precious.

'So we're trapped,' sighed Bergman.

'Not while we have Moonbase Alpha! Come on! Koenig said. 'Let's go home. Now that the machines of the Pirians are wrecked, there's nothing to hold the Moon in orbit around Piri. Let's move!' he called.

The Alphans moved purposefully towards the waiting Eagles.